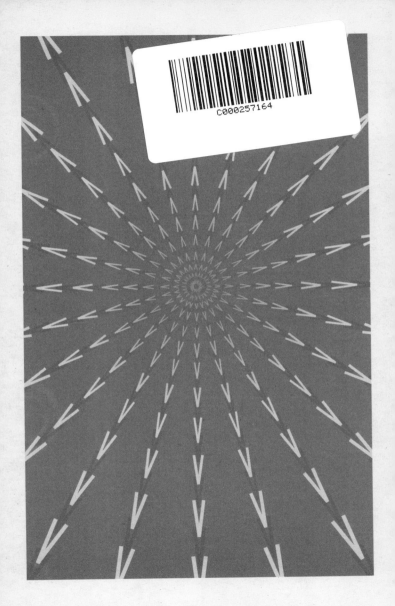

1 3 5 7 9 10 8 6 4 2

Vintage
20 Vauxhall Bridge Road,
London SW1V 2SA

Vintage Classics is part of the Penguin Random House
group of companies whose addresses can be found at
global.penguinrandomhouse.com

 Penguin
Random House
UK

First published in Great Britain by Jonathan Cape in 1996
This short edition published by Vintage in 2018

penguin.co.uk/vintage

A CIP catalogue record for this book is available from the British Library

ISBN 9781784874049

Typeset in 9.5/14.5 pt FreightText Pro
by Jouve (UK), Milton Keynes
Printed and bound by Clays Ltd, St Ives plc

Penguin Random House is committed to a sustainable future for
our business, our readers and our planet. This book is made from
Forest Stewardship Council® certified paper.

Rave

IRVINE WELSH

VINTAGE MINIS

Prologue

AH AM FUCKIN well fed up because there's nothing happening and ah've probably done a paracetamol but fuck it you need to have positive vibes and wee Amber, she's rubbing away at the back ay ma neck saying it'll happen when this operatic slab of synth seems to be 3D and ah realise that I'm coming up in a big way as that invisible hand grabs a hud ay me and sticks me onto the roof because the music is in me around me and everywhere, it's just leaking from my body, this is the game this is the game and ah look around and we're all going phoah and our eyes are just big black pools of love and energy and my guts are doing a big turn as the quease zooms through my body and we're up to the floor one by one and ah think I'm going tae need tae shit but ah hold on and it passes and I'm riding this rocket to Russia . . .

– No bad gear, eh, ah say tae Amber, as we dance ourselves slowly into it.

– Aye, sound.

– Awright, eh, says Ally.

Then it's ma main man on the decks, and he's on the form tonight, just pulling away at our collective psychic sex organs as they lay splayed out before us and ah get a big rosy smile off this goddess in a Lycra top, who, with her tanned skin and veneer of sweat, looks as enticing as a bottle of Becks from the cold shelf on a hot, muggy day, and my heart just goes bong bong bong Lloyd Buist reporting for duty, and the dance NRG the dance U4E ahhhh gets a hud ay me and I'm doing a sexy wee shuffle with Ally and Amber and Hazel and this big bone-heided cunt falls into me and gives me a hug and apologies and I'm slapping his hard wall of a stomach and thanking my lucky stars we're E'd and at this club and not pished at The Edge or somewhere brain-dead no that ah would touch that fuckin rubbish ... whoa rockets ... whoa it's still coming and I'm thinking *now* is the time to fall in love now now now but not with the world with that one special *her*, just do it, just do it now, just change your whole fuckin life in the space of a heartbeat, do it *now* ... but nah ... this is just entertainment ...

LATER IT'S TIME to chill at Hazel's gaff. Ally hits us all with some Slam which is all very nice except that he wants to spraff wildly and I'm in a dancy mood, naw, I'm in a shagging mood really. These Amsterdam Playboys do something tae ye behind your nuts. Woaf!

There are a lot of lassies back here. Ah love lassies

I'm thinking *now* is the time to fall in love now now now but not with the world with that one special *her*, just do it, just do it now, just change your whole fuckin life in the space of a heartbeat, do it *now* . . . but nah . . . this is just entertainment . . .

because they just look so fuckin brilliant, especially when you're E'd. It seems a wee bit obvious tae think that though, cause maist guys feel the same wey. Ah was reading somewhere about lassies being seen as either saints or whores. That's too simple . . . that sound's like shite to me. Maybe it was about laddies thinking of lassies in that way. Ah ask Ally about this.

– Naw, that's shite, man, much too simplistic, he says. Ally's got an amazing smile and his eyes seem to eat every word that comes from your mouth. – Ah've got ma ain classification, Lloyd. Lassies are either, one: Party Chicks; two: Straight-Pegs; three: Skankers; four: Party Chicks . . .

– You sais Party Chicks already but, ah told him.

– Let ays see . . . Party Chicks, Straight-Pegs, Skankers or Hounds, that's the four types ay bird, he smiles, casting his eyes round the room. – Maistly Party Chicks in here, thank fuck.

– So what dae ye class as a Party Chick?

– Fuck knows . . . it's obviously aw doon tae attitude, this whole classification . . . right . . . listen Lloyd, you necked that other pill yet?

Ah hadnae. Some crusties are burning incense in the corner and ah get a nice whiff which fills my nostrils and ah nod over at them. – Naw . . .

– Ye gaunny dae it soon?

– Naw . . . ah'm still up here, man. Ah might save it fir the fitba the morn, eh.

– Ah dinnae ken but eh, Lloyd . . . Ally pouts, looking like a toddler who's had his sweeties taken away.

– Fuck it, special occasion, eh, ah say to him, as either he or ah or some other cunt says every weekend as every weekend is, indeed, a special occasion. We neck our pills and the adrenalin rush of just having taken more chems has set Ally off again.

– Party Chicks can be subdivided, man, intae like two groups: Hiya Lassies and Sexy Feminists. Straight-Pegs are women who dinnae touch drugs, eh no man, and they shag only dull twats like themselves who are intae aw that home-and-garden shite. These are mainstream straight-pegs, man, dead easy tae spot. There are alternative straight-pegs, the kind ay po-faced feminists who read the *Guardian* or the *Independent* and that and are intae career-development paths and aw that sort ay shite. You have to watch them, if they arenae dykes, man, you can some-times mistake them for Sexy Feminists. No always, but sometimes.

This is magic. Ally's off. – The Boyle Laddie is off on a mazy! ah shout, and a few other people come over as Ally continues his rant.

– Hiya Lassies are the best but, man, but mair ay that in a bit. Skankers drink a lot ay alcohol and shag draftpak guys. They dress crassly, and seldom, if ever, touch Class As, although mair Skankers are daein them now. They're type of women whae go tae discos and dance around their handbags. Hounds are the lowest ay the low, man; they'll shag anything and are often alcoholics. Hiya Lassies are called so because they always say hi-ya-uh . . . when they meet you.

– You say that aw the time, Amber, Hazel says.

– So? Amber says, wondering what's going down.

– You have to watch though, Ally says to me, – because Skankers say this as well sometimes. It's the *wey* they say it that's important.

– Are you callin me a fuckin Skanker son? Amber asks Ally.

– Naw, man . . . you say hiya in a cool wey, he smiles at her and she melts. Fuck me if we arenae aw coming up again. – You're a Hiya Lassie, and they are easygoing, young, salt-of-the-earth Party Chicks. The best acquire that certain edge and become Sexy Feminists; the worst get stuck with a closet twat and become Straight-Pegs. Tell ye something else, Lloyd, he sais, turnin tae me, in eighty per cent ay cases the man always gets straight and boring before the woman.

– That's fuckin knob-cheese, Ally.

– Naw, Ally's right, somebody chips in. It's Nukes.

– See? It's just that you've picked boring women aw your life ya daft cunt! Ally smiles and gives me a big hug.

Foaahh . . . ah'm cunted here, ah feel like I'm shiting my soul out of every pore in my face. – Ah've goat tae dance through this one or ah'll sit cabbaged ay night . . . Nukes . . . help ays oan tae that flair, man . . .

– Ah'm blinded, man . . . blinded by the fuckin light . . .

wis that no a song by some cunt . . . goat tae sit doon, Nukes groaned, a magnificent aura rising from him. Ah staggered towards the speakers.

– Aw Lloyd, man, stey here n spraff a bit, Ally says, his pupils getting blacker but his lids getting heavier.

– In a bit, Ally. Ah feel that disco vibe. Rock the disco tek, eh.

Ah leave Ally to dance with Amber and her mate Hazel, two definite Party Chicks by any classification, who look as deliciously cool and colourful as a couple of happy-hour cocktails perched temptingly on the bar of Old Orleans. After a shuffle, my legs get moving and I'm enjoying it all. More strange things start happening behind my genitals. Ah remember ah fired intae Amber at a party last year and looking at her made me wonder why ah hadnae done it again. Ah say to Amber first, – Listen, fancy hitting the bedroom for a meeting of, minds and the other bits?

– No, I'm no into sex with you. Ah fancy firing right intae Ally later on, he looks so fucking gorgeous.

– Yeah, yeah, yeah, ah smile, and ah look over at Ally with his Tenerife tan and have to admit that the cunt does look, eh, a wee bitty more than presentable; mind you, every cunt does on E. He's gesturing over and I'm waving back at him. A big white

Not a whitey, though heartbeat, perspiration and heating have all definitely increased. Hit the Volvic. Can you feel it, crew!

– Fucking good tape, Ambs . . . make ays a copy . . . is it Slam? Is it?

She closes her eyes and then opens them briefly and nods at me seriously, – Jist a Yip Yap mixed tape, eh.

Whoa, yes to fuck . . .

– I'm up for it, Haze says to me.

– Eh?

– A shag, like. That's what you were talking to Ambs aboot, eh. You and me, then. The bedroom.

Ah was going to get round to asking her before ah goat diverted by . . . let's just see . . . before ah was diverted by Amber's KB; whoa ya fucker am ah in touch with my feelings or what, but it's all right and ah shout: – Hey Ally, ah'm sexually jealous of you, and he pouts and comes over and gives me a hug and Amber does too so ah should feel good but ah feel a bit of a cunt for making them feel bad because ah discover that I'm no really sexually jealous of Ally who's a smashing lad as Gordon McQueen on *Scotsport* would say but only he's no oan it now it's that Gerry McNee gadge that gets tae say it now, and the other radge who writes aboot the fitba n aw that's on it as well, but as they boys would say: ah wish him every success, etc., etc.

– Amber's saying she's intae firing intae ye, ah tell Ally.

Amber smiles and pushes me in the chest. Ally turns to me and says, – The important thing, man, is that ah love Amber, he wraps his arm around her. – What happens sexually . . . that's just detail. The important thing is, man, that ah love everybody that ah know in this room. And ah know everybody! Except these boys, he points to the crusties who are skinning up in the corner. But ah'd love these cunts as well if ah knew them. Ninety per cent of people are loveable, man, once ye get tae ken them . . . if they believe in themselves enough . . . if they love and respect themselves, eh . . .

Ah feel ma face opening up like a tin ay sardines as ah give Ally a smile and then ah turn to Haze and say, – Let's go for it . . .

In the bedroom Hazel struggles out of her kit and ah get out of mine and we're under the duvet. It's too hot to be under the duvet but this in case any cunt comes in, which they will. We've got the tongues working hard and I probably taste very salty and sweaty cause she does. It takes me yonks tae get an erection, but that doesnae bother ays because I'm mair intae the touching oan E than the penetration. She's gaun pretty radge though and ah manage tae bring her off using my fingers. Ah'm just lying their watching her orgasm like ah was watching her score for Hibs. We'll just play that one back again, Archie . . . I want it tae happen for her seven times. After a while, though, ah start to feel something happen and ah have tae stop and get out and rummage through my jeans.

– What is it? She asks, – I've got a condom here . . .

– Naw, it's the nitrate like, the poppers. Ah find the bottle. It's got soas ah don't get anything out of the shagging now without the amyl nitrate. Es are mair sensual than sexual, but you've got to have the nitrate though, man, no really an optional extra, now really as essential as a cock or a fanny like.

So well, so well, we're still playing skin games and this is so good cause I'm still rushing and the tactile sensitivity has been increased a mere tenfold by the ecky and our skins are so sensitive it's like we can just reach inside each other and caress all those internal bits and pieces and we work ourselves round into the sixty-nine and as ah start licking and she does there's no way that I, at any rate, am no going to come quickly so we break off and ah get on top and inside her and then she's on top of me and then I'm on top of her and then she's on top of me, but it's a bit too much theatrics from her, ah suspect; could be wrong, perhaps she's just inexperienced because she must only be about eighteen or something when I'm thirty fucking one which is possibly too old to be carrying on like this when ah could be married to a nice fat lady in a nice suburban house with children and a steady job where ah have urgent reports to write informing senior management that unless certain action is taken the organisation could suffer, but it's me and Purple Haze here together, fuck sake

and now it's getting better, more relaxed, soulful. It's getting good . . .

. . . it's fine fine fine and Haze and ah spill fluids in and over each other and I'm sticking the amyl nitrate up her nose and mines and we're holding onto that high crashing wave of an orgasm together

WHOA HO HO

HO HO

HO

OOOHHHHHOOOOOOOOOOOOOOHHHHHHH HHHHHHHOOOOOOOOOOOOOOOOOOOOOHH HHHHHHHHHHHHHH!!!!!!!!!!!!!!!!!!!

Ah like the after-feeling with my heart pumping from orgasm and nitrate. It's barry feeling ma body readjust, ma heartbeat slow doon.

– That was brilliant! Hazel says.

– It was . . . ah try tae find the words, – fruity. A full, fruit-flavoured one.

Ah wonder if anyone will be up for cocktails at Old Orleans later today or tomorrow night, or is it now tonight?

We talk for a bit, and then join the others. It's really weird how you can be so intimate with someone you dinnae really ken on E. Ah dinnae really ken Hazel, but you can have a barry ride oaf ay a stranger oan ecky. It takes a long time tae get that intimate oan straight street. Ye huv tae build up tae it, eh.

Ally's right over to me. – That wee Hazel, a total wee doll. Dirty cunt man, you, eh. Fuck sake, Lloyd, ah wish ah wis sixteen now and had aw this. Punk and that, that was shite compared tae this . . .

Ah look at him and then look around the room, – But

ye have got it, ya daft cunt, just like you had punk, just like
ye'll have the next thing that comes along, cause you
refuse tae grow up. Ye just like tae have yir cake n eat it.
It's the only fuckin way, man.

– Nae point in huvin yir cake if ye cannae fuckin well
scran it back, eh, no?

– This is brilliant . . . how wis Tenerife by the way? Ye
never really telt ays.

– Ace, man. Better than Ibiza. Ah'm no jokin. Ye
should've come, Lloyd. You'd have lapped it up.

– Ah really wanted tae, Ally, but the hireys fucked it
but, eh. Cannae save, that's ma problem. What aboot John
Bogweed last week? How wis that?

– John Bigheid? Shite.

– Aye.

– Happens though, eh.

– Aye . . . jist nivir goat intae the stuff eh wis playin . . .
mind you, some ay it wis awright . . . you're a dirty cunt . . .

– Ah know, ah know. You should fire intae Amber. She's
up fir ye, man.

– Fuck Lloyd, man, ah cannae be bothered shaggin
Amber. I've started tae feel bad aboot chasin wee dolls,
fillin thir heids wi shite and knobbing them, then runnin
like fuck until the weekend, man. Ah feel like ah'm between
fourteen and sixteen years auld again, when it was just a
shag tae try and get it over wi as soon as possible. Headin
straight back tae the first stage ay sexual development, me,
eh, man.

– Ah aye, what's the next stage?

– Ye take your time, gie the lassie a good feel, try to get her tae come, find clitoris, try oral sex . . . that wis me fae aboot sixteen tae aboot eighteen. Then eftir that, fae aboot eighteen tae aboot twenty one, it wis eywis positions wi me. Dae it different weys, try different approaches like doggy style, on chairs, up the erse and aw that sort of stuff, sort ay sexual gymnastics. The next stage was tae find a lassie and try tae tune intae each other's internal rhythms. Make music thegither. The thing is, Lloyd, ah think ah've passed that stage and ah'm headin back in the full circle when ah want tae go forward.

– Maybe yuv jist covered everything, ah venture.

– Naw, he snaps, – no way. Ah want that kind ay psychic communion, gittin right inside each other's nut, like astral flight and that. He presses his forefinger onto my head. – And that period is now until I find it. Never had it, man. Had the internal rhythms, but no the joining ay the souls. Never even came close. The eckies help, but the only way you can get the joining ay the souls is if you let her into your head and she lets you into hers, at the same time. It's communication, man. You can't get that with any Party Chick, even when you're both E'd up. It has to be love. That's what ah'm really lookin for, Lloyd: love.

Ah smile into his big eyes and say, – Yir a fuckin sexual philosopher, Mister Boyle.

– Naw ah'm no jokin. Ah'm lookin for love.

– Maybe that's what we're all really looking for, Ally.

– The thing is Lloyd, man, mibee ye cannae look fir it. Mibee it hus tae find you.

– Aye, but until ye do, ye want a fuckin good ride but, eh.

LATER ON, AMBER tearfully tells me that Ally's rejected her and won't sleep with her cause he doesnae love her as a lover, just as a pal. Nukes is in the kitchen with us and he just throws his hands up as if this is aw too heavy and says, – Ah'm away ... see yis ... But ah notice that the cunt has left wi this lassie, and this is the cue for everybody to head off but ah stay back and try to explain Ally's stance to Amber and Hazel and do some lines of coke with her and we watch the sun come up and discuss everything. Hazel goes through to bed but Amber wants to stay up talking. Eventually, though, she falls asleep on the couch. Ah go through to another bedroom and get a quilt and put it over her. She looks peaceful. She needs a boyfriend: a nice young guy who'll look after her and let her look after him. Ah think about getting intae bed with Hazel and crashing but ah could feel the distance growing between us with the MDMA running down in our bodies. Ah head hame and although I'm not religious ah pray for a boyfriend for Amber and a special girlfriend each for Ally and me. I'm not religious but ah just like the idea ay friends hoping for good things for each other; like the idea of all this goodwill floating around in psychic space.

Back hame ah neck two eggs and wash them down with a bottle of Becks. Ah stagger tae bed where a strange, disturbed sleep descends on me. Ah'm in Cunt City's familiar district of Shag-You-Up-The-Fuckin-Hole.

1

MY HEAD IS a bit fucked; basically cause ah took a couple ay jellies tae come doon. Stupidity and sleaze, that's what it is. Schemie windows. Ah look at the world through schemie windows. The phone rings by the bed. Nukes is on the other end of the line.

– Lloyd . . . it's me.

– Nukes. Awright. Recovered fae last night, or wis it this mornin? Ah cannae git gaun, man. Took a couple ay these fuckin jellies tae come doon . . .

– Tell ays aboot it. Ye gaun tae the fitba?

– Naw . . . ah fancy a pint.

– Ah'm intae seein what the view's like fae the new stands, eh.

– Fuck the new stands up the hole, man.

– They look awright but . . . fuckin better than the Jambo's shite.

– Aye, cheap B&Q flatpack rubbish. Gary MacKay knocked them up when thir wis nae fitba oan Sky one night. Dinnae ken if ah could sit in the one place for ninety minutes but, Nukes . . .

– Awright then chavvy, we'll keep oor options open . . .

– Sound.

– Right, see ye in The Windsor in half an hour. Dinnae phone up Ally but. If ah hear that cunt spraffin oan again aboot how good Jon Digweed wis the other week, or aboot how brilliant Tenerife is, ah'll throw the cunt in front ay a bus.

– Right . . . that chancin cunt telt me Digweed wis shite.

– The cunt sais the same aboot Tony Humphries. Eh eywis starts the night by saying everything's shite. Later oan ye hear um tell some cunt it wis no bad and then, by the end ay the night, aw eh kin talk aboot is how brilliant it wis.

Ah take a shower and try tae get moving. These fuckin jellies: never again. Ah stagger out up the Walk tae meet Nukes. We go off on the pish. We take a couple ay jellies each to save money. Nukes had a sound argument: – Ye get the same effect with a couple ay jellies and four pints that you would get fae thirty pints. Why gie they brewer cunts the money and waste time?

The afternoon dissolves into a sludgy evening. – Ah'm fucked, man, ah say to Nukes. Ah drift off intae the City Of The Cunted, Noddyland, and get shaken back intae Planet Leith by the barman. He's saying something but ah can't make out what it is. Ah wobble along out the door. Ah can hear Nukes singing Hibs songs but ah can't see the cunt.

Ye get the same effect with a couple ay jellies and four pints that you would get fae thirty pints. Why gie they brewer cunts the money and waste time?

Ah dinnae ken whair we are, we seem tae be up the toon. Ah hear people laughing at me, sort of posh voices. Then I'm in this taxi and I'm in another pub in Leith. Ah hear a guy shouting at me, – That was the cunt that shagged his sister, and ah tried to say something but ah was too drunk, and ah hear another guy saying, – Naw, he's Lloyd Buist, Vaughan Buist's brother, eh mate. You're thinkin ay the other Lloyd, Lloyd Beattie that boy's name wis.

– Dinnae tell ays thirs two fuckin Lloyds in Leith, one guy sais.

Next thing ah know is that I'm talking to ma mate Woodsy, whae ah havenae seen in yonks, and he's gaun oan about God, drink and E. He takes me back to his and ah crash.

2

AH WOKE UP on Woodsy's couch feeling shitey. Ah was
sick, with a dentist-drill headache and my lip was burst
and swollen and ah had like a nasty smudged bit of purple
black mascara under my right eye. This reminded me why
ah took Class As instead of alcohol. Ah mind ay Nukes and
me paggering. Fuck knows whether it was wi each other
or some other fucker. Given the slightness of my wounds
it was probably some other fucker cause Nukes is a hard
cunt and would have done me a lot more damage.

– You fucked it up goodstyle last night, eh? Woodsy
said, bringing me a cup of tea.

– Aye, ah said, still too out off it to feel too apologetic,
– Nukes n me hit the satellite tellies and went for it. Ended
up in some brawl.

– Youse cunts are fuckin crazy. Alcohol's Satan's
instrument, man. As fir jellies . . . well, it's no often that ah
agree wi that poofy wee Tory cunt on the telly . . . but
fuckin hell, man, ah expect such behaviour fae Nukes,

him being a cashie n that, but ah thought you'd have a wee bit mair savvy, Lloyd.

– Aw Woodsy, man, ah pleaded. That cunt Woodsy was still on this religion kick. He'd kept at it, mind you, it was last summer when it began. The cunt had claimed to have seen God after two Supermarios and two snowballs at the outdoor Rezurrection. We dumped him in the Garage Room tae chill, he seemed tae be overheating badly. Ah stuck a Volvic in his hand and left him to the pink ele-phants. Wrong really, but ah was so fucking up and the light show was so phenomenal in the main tent that ah wanted tae get back to the action. Two maternalish Party Chicks kept an indulgent eye on him.

The careplan fucked up when Woodsy's queasy attack necessitated him leaving the Party Chicks and heading for the chemical bogs to converse with the big aluminium telephone. It was in one of those putrid traps that he met the Big Chief.

The worst thing was that God apparently told him that Ecstasy was His gift to those in the know, who then had the duty to spread the word. He apparently instructed Woodsy to set up a Rave Gospel club.

Now ah didnae ken whether or no Woodsy's head had fried, or he was on some self-important control kick; per-haps a Koresh-style scam to access as many Party Chicks as required. Are you receiving me, girls? Are you really ready to receive me, and all that head-fucking schissee, shit, merde, shite. Whatever, he was picking the wrong drug for a control freak. The only person you can control on E is yourself. Koresh wouldn't have lasted five minutes if he had his posse E'd in Waco. Cut the fuckin religious shit, Davey ma man, we came to dance . . .

– Listen, Lloyd, you still goat they Technics decks at yours?

– Aye, bit thir Shaun's like. Jist till eh comes back fae Thailand, eh.

Shaun was gaunny be away for a year, but if he had any sense he'd stey away for good, and Shaun was a sharp cunt. He'd teamed up with this guy from Lancashire called The Crow, and they had made a small fortune screwing rich cunt's hooses. They had wisely decided tae call it quits before they did that one job too many and hit the trail to Thailand via Goa. Nice for them and nice for me as ah inherited the decks and Shaun's record collection which boasted some ice-cool soul rarities.

– Ye must be gitting quite good oan them, eh?

– Awright, aye, ah lied. Ah'd only been looking after the decks for a couple of months. Ah had nae sense ay timing, nae motor skills and no a great deal ay vinyl. Ah had wanted tae practise oan them mair, but ah had been doing some joinery work on the side with my mate Drewsy and ah was daein quite a bit ay dealing for The Poisonous Cunt.

– Look, Lloyd, ah've goat this gig organised at the Reck-Tangle Club in Pilton. Ah want you oan the bill. You first, then me. What dae ye think?

– When's this?

– Next month. The fourteenth. It's a while likes.

– Sound. Count ays in.

Ah was shite on the decks but ah reasoned that a deadline would force ays tae get my act thegither. Ah wisnae so chuffed when Woodsy telt me he wanted samplings of hymns and gospel music mixed intae techno, house, garage and ambient stuff, but ah was still up for it.

Anyway, ah decided tae spend a lot of time at home with the decks. A lot ay my mates, especially Nukes, Ally and Amber, were pretty supportive. They came round for a blow, and often brought dance records they'd borrowed. Ah started going tae a few clubs straight to watch the DJs and see what they did. My favourite was Craig Smith, the Edinburgh DJ at Solefusion, who always seemed to be having loads of fun with what he was doing. Too many seemed po-faced cunts with no spirit, and it showed in the Richard Millhouse. Ye cannae gie other cunts enjoyment if you cannae enjoy it yourself.

ONE AFTERNOON AH was settling down to a bit of Richard Nixon when the door went. Ah had the music on low, but ah still thought it was the yuppie cunts across the landing who complained about anything and everything.

Ah opened the door and before me stood auld Mrs McKenzie from doonstairs. – Soup, she spat out, her face screwed up.

Ah remembered. Ah had forgotten to go to the

supermarket to get ingredients for a pot of soup. Ah always make a big pot on a Thursday before the weekend ay abuse starts so ah know I've got something nutritious in if I'm too fucked or skint tae dae anything else. Ah take auld Mrs McKenzie some doon in a tupperware bowl. She's a nice auld cunt, but what started off as a one-off gesture of goodwill has now evolved into custom and practice and it's starting tae fracture ma tits tae pieces.

– Sorry, Mrs Mack, no had a chance tae make it yit eh no.

– Aye . . . ah jist thought . . . soup . . . the laddie upstairs usually brings doon a bowl ay soup oan a Thursday . . . ah wis jist tellin Hector. Soup . . . ah wis jist sayin tae Hector the other day. Soup. The laddie up the stairs. Soup.

– Aye, ah'll be makin it in a bit.

– Soup soup soup . . . ah thought we'd be gittin some soup.

– It's aw in hand, Mrs Mack, ah kin assure ye ay that.

– Soup . . .

– THE SOUP ISN'T READY YET MISSUS MCKEN-ZIE. WHEN I'VE MADE IT, WHICH WILL BE LATER ON TODAY, I SHALL BRING SOME DOWN TO YOU. OKAY?

– Soup. Later on.

– THAT'S IT, MISSUS MCKENZIE. SOUP. LATER ON.

Ah must have been making a racket cause the Straight-Peg woman across the way comes tae her door to investigate the noise. – Are you okay, Mrs McKenzie? Did the noise from that music disturb you too? she asks the auld dear, the fuckin self-centred manipulative soulless cunt.

– The soup's comin, Mrs Mack said, cheerful and appeased as she moved painstakingly slowly along the landing and down the stairs.

Ah went back inside, wrapped it on the Richard and headed oot tae the shops tae get the ingredients for the soup. As ah left there was a message on the answer-machine. It was a long rambling statement fae Nukes that actually said nothing except that he had his hoose raided by the polis.

3

WHEN AH GOT back from the supermarket with the soup ingredients, ah was just in the door when the bell behind me sounded tersely. It was The Poisonous Cunt and she was in tow with The Victim whose coupon was fixed in a nervous, tense stare which even my most open smile couldn't break down.

The Victim was a chronic fuck-up. People like her always seemed to hang out with The Poisonous Cunt. In turn, she kept their self-esteem low and made sure that they stayed in psychic immiseration. She was a curator of dead souls. It concerned me that ah seemed tae be spending more time with The Poisonous Cunt; we just turned each other onto suppliers of drugs, and good deals. Ah had once shagged The Victim, when ah was coked up ah bullshitted her intae bed one night . . . intae bed, my arse, it was actually onto the flair, the flair behind the couch where Ally was shagging this lassie he'd met at Pure. Anyway, The Victim gave ays hassle for weeks after, with phone calls, at clubs, etc. She had a tendency to put up with anything, and was into any form of attention. That was why she eywis ended up in abusive relationships.

– Diddly dit dit dee, two ladies, ah sang at them with a cheerfulness ah didnae feel as ah ushered them in, only to be met with frost. The Poisonous Cunt rolled her bottom lip downwards like an inverted red carpet. She had that fatigued, irritated air of a young woman who had seen more than she should but had not yet seen what she wanted, and had just about decided to wrap it rather than look further.

– Wait here, she snapped at The Victim who began to softly bubble. Ah went over tae do a bit of token stagey comforting, but The Poisonous Cunt wrenched my arm and pulled me into the kitchen, shutting the door behind us and lowering her voice so much that ah could only see her lips move.

– Eh? ah asked her.

– She's fucked up.

– What's new? ah shrugged, but ah don't think The Poisonous Cunt heard ays.

– She's deluding herself, ah told that to her, she said, sucking on a fag and contorting her face in a mask of hateful contempt. – You're fuckin well livin in a fool's paradise, hen, ah said tae her, Lloyd. But she widnae listen. Now she's getting it aw back. And who's the first one she comes runnin tae?

– Right . . . right . . . ah nodded as empathetically as ah

could, loading my food from the shopping bag into the cupboard and fridge.

– She misses fuckin periods aw the time and goes through this 'I'm up the stick' shite. Ah felt like saying to her: you cannae get up the stick when he's shagging you up the arse, but ah didnae. Ah felt like saying tae her: the reason you always miss periods is because you're fucked up in the heid, hen; your life's a mess and if you're that fucked in the heid it's bound tae tell on yir body.

– Ah see, ah see . . . her and Bobby again . . .

The Victim's current principal exploiter was a crazy biker guy called Bobby who ah'd known for years. Bobby had a split personality. One side of him was pure evil, the other completely cuntish.

– But ah bit ma tongue. Thing is, Lloyd, he came roond and started playin mind games wi her. Solo wis just fuckin laughin, so we had tae get oot. We just want tae sit here and chill for a bit until that bastard Bobby goes.

– Look, that's sound by me, but ye'll huv tae dae it alaine, eh. Ah'm meetin this boy whaes supposed tae have some ay they pink champagnes, the speedballs, ken?

– Git me five . . . naw, six . . . she rasped, rummaging through her bag for her purse.

– That's if ehs goat thum likes, ah said, taking her money. Ah wasnae gaunnae try and score, ah was just going to my brother's for a scran. It wasnae just because it didnae sound cool enough tae tell The Poisonous Cunt that; it was because she was a nasty, nosey bastard and ah didnae want her kennin too much aboot ays.

Ah left them to it, clocking The Victim's arse in her black stretch leggings before ah left, both strangely pleased and disappointed no tae feel any reaction whatsoever.

AH TOOK THE bus at the fit ay the Walk tae ma brother Vaughan's. Ah was a bit late. When ah got there, ah had to ring for ages. Vaughan was out and Fiona, my sister-in-law, was in the back playing with my niece, Grace, who was two and a bit of nutter, like two year aulds are.

– Lloyd! ah thought it was you. Come in, come in.

Ah clocked that Vaughan had been at the decorating but ah didnae say anything. The hoose was furnished in tasteless Habitat country-style, ridiculous in a suburban semi. That was Vaughan and Fiona. Ah love them in a strange way – a tense, dutiful love – but you cannae say nowt tae cunts like that about taste. It just isnae an issue with them. It comes oot the page ay a catalogue.

Ah asked Fiona if ah could use the phone and she took the hint and took Grace out into the gairdin. Ah called Nukes. – What's the story? ah asked him.

– That's me finished wi the cashies and the collies. Ah'm a marked man now, Lloyd. Polis doon here the other night accusin ays ay sorts ay things, man. Well oot ay order.

– Ye git charged?

– Naw, but it shit ays up. Some ay the boys say no tae

worry, but fuck that, man. Ah'm daein a bit ah dealin and that could be three fuckin years oot ma life jist for a bit ay swedgin at the fitba.

– Ah wis gaunnae ask if you could punt some stuff fir ays n aw . . .

– No way. Low profile for a while, that's me.

– Awright then. Come doon fir a blow next week but, eh.

– Awright.

– Cheers, Nukes . . . eh, ye mind ay what happened the other night? Did we git intae some bother?

– Ye dinnae want tae ken, Lloyd.

– Nukes . . .

The line clicked dead.

That was me para as fuck, but no as para as Nukes. Something was bugging the cunt bigtime. Ah knew that Nukes wasnae so intae the casuals these days, but he still got it together for the odd big swedge. Ah could never understand the attraction, but he swore by the rush. If he's kent by the polis, though, that's bad news; when you're holding just a few drugs for you and your mates, they call you a dealer. He was being sensible, n ah resolved that ah was going tae try tae take it easy n aw for a bit.

– Like the new colour? Fiona asks.

Grace climbed up on me and tried to push my eyeball out of its socket. Ah removed her hand before she could go for my other eye, the one that was bruised. – Aye, it's sound. Very relaxing. Ah wis jist gaunnae say, ah lied. – Ye must have been keepin Vaughan busy, eh, no? Where is eh?

Grace climbed down and ran over to Fiona and wrapped herself around her leg.

– Three guesses, Fiona smiled in the kind of way that changed her from being a young housewife into a shag.

– The boolin? ah asked.

– Right first time, she nodded wearily. – He said to tell you to meet him doon thair for a pint. The dinner'll no be ready till five.

– Sound . . . ah said. It wisnae really sound. Ah would rather have stayed with Fiona and Grace than listened to Vaughan's shite. – . . . eh, but maybe I'll jist chill here for a bit.

– Lloyd, I've got loads to do. I don't want you under my feet, one bairn's enough, she smirked.

– Thanks a lot, ah laughed, pretending at being hurt. We continued with this ritual. It was pathetic and dull, but it often gave me a strange, queasy feeling of exhilaration to talk bland shite with people and not worry about being a smart cunt simply because you were linked in some way to each other. It was a wild trip.

Too much ay this shite can fuck a cunt's heid but, and after a while ah decided ah'd better go and see Vaughan.

IT WAS A pretty glorious summer's evening when ah got out in the street. Ah found myself with a strange spring in my step. Of course, it was Thursday. Last weekend's drugs had been well and truly processed by now, the toxins discharged: sweated, shat and pished out; the hangover finito; the psychological self-loathing waning as the chemistry of the brain de-fucked itself and the fatigue sinking into the past as the old adrenalin pump starts slowly getting back into gear in preparation for the next round ay abuse. This feeling, when you've cracked the depressive hangover and the body and mind is starting to fire up again, is second only to coming up on a good E.

AT THE CLUB, Vaughan's playing bools with this old cunt. He nods at me, and the auld cunt looks up with a slightly tetchy stare and ah realise that I've broken his concentration by casting my shadow over his line of vision. Steeling himself, the auld codger lets the bool roll, roll, roll and I'm thinking he's gone too far out, but naw, the wily auld cunt kens the score because the bool does a Brazilian spin, that's what it does, a fuckin Brazilian spin, and it comes back like a fuckin boomerang and slips like a surreptitious queue-jumper in behind Vaughan's massed lines of defence, rolling up to the jack and sneaking it away.

Ah cheer the auld gadge for that shot. Vaughan has his last one but ah decide no tae watch it but to go in and get some drinks. Ah discover I've a wrap of speed in my pocket, left over from fuck knows when. Ah take it to the bog, and chop it out into some lines on the cistern. If I'm gaunny have to talk bools ah might as well fuckin go for it in a big way ... Ah come out, charged up to fuck. Ah remember this gear, dabbing away at it the other week. It's much better to snort though, this stuff.

– Didnae stay for the climax, Vaughan says, looking deflated. – Could have done wi yir support fir that last shot thair.

– Sorry, Vaughan, ah wis burstin fir a tropical fish, eh. Did ye git it?

– Naw, eh wis miles oot! The auld cunt roars. The auld cunt is dressed in white slacks, a blue open-necked shirt and has a sunhat on.

Ah slap the auld cunt on the back, – Nice one there, mate! Brilliant shot by the way, that wee spinner that nicked it at the end. Ah'm Lloyd, Vaughan's brother.

– Aye Lloyd, ah'm Eric, he extends his hand and gies ays a crushing masonic grip, – ye play the bools yersel?

– Naw, Eric, naw ah dinnae, mate; it's no really ma scene, ken. Ah mean ah'm no knockin the game n that, a great game . . . ah mean ah wis chillin oot the other day watchin that Richard Corsie gadge oan the box . . . he used tae be wi the *Post*, did eh no? That boy kens how tae fling a bool . . .

Fuck me, this Lou Reed is hitting the mark quickstyle.

– Eh, what yis wantin? Vaughan shouts, a wee bit embarrassed at ma ranting.

– Naw naw naw, ah'll git them. Three lager, is it no?

– Poof's pish, Eric scoffs, – make mine Special.

– A special drink for a special victory, eh, Eric, ah smile. The auld cunt gie ays one back. – Yuv goat Vaughan's puss seekint here right enough!

– Aye, right, Vaughan goes, – are you gaunnae git them in, or what?

Ah hit the bar and the guy behind says that you have to have a tray to get served, and ah joke that I've got enough to carry as it is and he says something short like house rules, but a wee cunt in the queue hands me one anyway. I've forgotten about all the daft fuckin rules they have in places like this, the Brylcreemed cunts wi their blazers wi the club badges on them and how at closing time there's mair falling masonry than when the Luftwaffe bombed Coventry cathedral . . . and now I'm back at my seat.

– Cheers, boys! ah say, raising my pint, – Tell ye what, Eric, ah knew that you had the bools after seeing ye in action there. This gadge has bools, ah telt masel. That Brazilian spin, man! Whoa, ya cunt that ye fuckin well are!

– Aye, said Eric, smugly, – it wis a wee thing ah thought ah'd try. Ah said tae masel, Vaughan's marshalled his defences well, but, ah thought, try a wee sneaky one roond the backdoor, and it just might come off.

– Aye, it wis a good shot, Vaughan conceded.

– It wis fuckin ace, ah told him. – You've heard of total fitba, the Dutch invented it, right? Well this man here, ah nodded towards Eric, – is total bools. You could've went for the blast there, Eric, tried that Premier League style huffing and puffing but naw, a bit ay class, a bit ay art.

The pint was drained. Vaughan hit the bar.

This was always a thing with Vaughan when he met me. He had a sense of duty, of the responsibilities ay a married man and a parent, so that whenever he did have an allocated time he would try tae squeeze as many units of alcohol into it as he possibly could. And he could drink. Thank fuck it was draught Becks ah was on. Ah wouldnae touch any Scottish shite, especially McEwan's lager, the vile toxic pish that it is, for anything. The pints kept flowing and this speed was still digging in, and ah was almost hyperventilating. The thing is, it was like auld Eric got dragged in by the vibe, by the exuberance, and it was like the auld bastard had snorted a few lines n aw.

After a quick draining of the next pint he came back wi some mair beers, wi nips as chasers.

– Fuckin hell! ah said. – Expect the unexpected wi this man, eh?

– Aye, too right, Vaughan smiled. Vaughan was looking at us both with a big, indulgent those-are-mad-cunts-but-I-love-them smile. It made me feel close to him.

– Ye should go up n see Ma n Dad, Vaughan told me.

– Aye, ah guiltily conceded, – ah've been meanin tae drop by this tape ah made up for them. Motown, eh.

– Good. They'll appreciate that.

– Aye, Marvin, Smokey, Aretha n aw that, ah said, then promptly changed the subject, turnin tae Eric, – Listen, Eric, that stunt you pulled wi the bools, ah began.

– Aye, Eric cut in, – fair took the wind oot ay Vaughan here's sails, that's if ye dinnae mind ays sayin like, Vaughan! Eric laughed. – Expect the unexpected!

– Do-do-do-do, do-do-do-do, ah start the *Twilight Zone* theme tune, then ah think of something, – Listen,

Eric, your second name isnae Cantona, by any chance, is it?

– Eh naw, Stewart, he said.

– It's just that there wis a Cantonaesque quality aboot that final shot thair, ah began giggling, a real dose ay the Flight Lieutenants, and Eric did too, – it fair blew fuckin Vaughan Ryan's Express right out the water . . .

– Aye . . . awright then, ya cunts, Vaughan sulked.

– Ooh ah, Cantona, ah started, and Eric joined in. A few groups of drinkers and auld couples looked over at us.

Encouraged, auld Eric and ah were up doing the can-can: na, na na, na na na na na na na, na, na na, na na na na na na . . .

– Hey, come oan now, that's enough. Thir's folk here tryin tae enjoy a drink, a mumpy cunt with a blazer and badge moans.

– Aye, well nae herm done! auld Eric shouts back, then says in lower voice tae us, but still enough for every cunt tae hear, – What's his fuckin problem?

– C'moan Eric . . . Vaughan goes, – Lloyd's no a member here.

– Aye, well, the laddie's been signed in. Signed in as a guest. It's aw bona fide. Wir no daein herm. Like ah sais, nae herm done, Eric shook his heid.

– Procedures have been observed, eh, Eric, ah smirk.

– The situation's completely bona fide, Eric confirms stoically.

– Ah think a certain Monsieur Vaughan Buist may be

smarting over a recent sporting setback, n'est-ce pas, Monsieur Cantona? He ees, ow you say, ay leetal peesed off.

– Je suis une booler, Eric cackles.

– It's no that, Lloyd, Vaughan mumps, – Aw ah'm tryin tae say is thit you're no a member here. Yir a guest. Yir the responsibility ay the people that bring ye. That's aw ah'm tryin tae say.

– Aye . . . bit nae herm done . . . mumbles Eric.

– It's jist like that club you go tae, Lloyd. That place up at The Venue. What's that club called?

– The Pure.

– Aye, right. It's like if you're at The Pure n ah wis tae come up n you were tae sign ays in . . .

– As ma guest, ah snorted, laughing uncontrollably at the thought. Ah heard auld Eric start as well. It got soas we were gaunnae peg oot.

– As your guest . . . Vaughan had started now. Ah thought: this is me fucked. Flight Lieutenant Biggles, hovering over the grim metropolis of Cunt City . . . Auld Eric started wheezing, as Vaughan carried on, – as the guest of one's brother Lloyd at the exclusive club in town he frequents . . .

We were interrupted by a choking sound as auld Eric boaked thin beer-sick over the table. The humpty cunt with the blazer and badge was right over to him and grabbed up his pint. – That's it! Oot, c'moan! Oot!

Vaughan grabbed the pint back. – That's no fuckin well it at aw, Tommy.

– Aye it bloody well is! That's it, the humpty cunt snapped.

– Dinnae fuckin well come ower tae this table n say that's it, Vaughan said, – cause that's no it at aw.

Ah slapped Eric on the back and helped the auld cunt to his feet and through to the lavvy. – It's a sair ficht, right enough, ah caught him gasp between mouthfuls of sick as he spewed up into the bog pan.

– Aye, Eric, yir awright, man. Nae danger, ah said encouragingly. Ah felt like ah was at Rez, talking Woodsy down when he had his freak-out, but here ah was with a daft auld cunt in a bowling club.

WE GOT ERIC hame. It was an auld hoose where the door led straight oantae the main road. We propped him against it and rang the bell and moved away. A woman answered and pulled him in and slammed the door shut. Ah heard the sound of blows and Eric's screams from behind the door, – Dinnae, Betty . . . ah'm sorry, Betty . . . dinnae hit ays again . . .

Then we went back tae Vaughan's. The meal was a bit dried oot, and Fiona wisnae pleased at our state. Ah didnae want tae eat anything, but ah scranned with fake enthusiasm.

Ah felt heavy and embarrassed and ah left early, opting tae walk doon tae the port. As ah was coming doon Leith Walk, ah saw The Poisonous Cunt on the other side. Ah crossed over.

– Where ye gaun? ah asked.

– Just gaun back tae yours. Ah phoned Solo and he wanted ays tae pick up some stuff for him. You're pished!

– A bit, aye.

– Did ye git the speedballs?

Ah looked at her for a bit. – Naw . . . ah didnae see the boy, eh. Ah ran intae some cunt, eh no. Ah had a sudden twinge of fear. – Whaire's The Victim?

– Still at yours.

– Fuck!

– What is it?

– The Victim's bulimic! She'll clean oot aw that fuckin shoppin! Ye shouldnae huv left her oan her ain!

We hurried back to find that The Victim had eaten and vomited up the three raw cauliflowers ah had earmarked for Mrs McKenzie's soup.

Ah had to hit the Asians for some rotting overpriced ingredients – but fair enough ah suppose as the cunts've pulled ays oot a hole wi bevvy and skins many times – and then it took me ages, half pished, tae make the soup. The Poisonous Cunt had some tabs ay acid which she gave me in lieu of cash the scabby hoor owed ays. – Go lightly wi this stuff, Lloyd, it's the fucking business.

She played around on the decks with the phones for a while. Ah had to admit it, The Poisonous Cunt wisnae that bad, she seemed to have a good feel for it. Ah noted that she had a ring through her navel, exposed as it was by her short T-shirt. – Cool ring, ah shouted at her, and she gave me the thumbs-up and did a strange wee dance and flashed me a weird, ugly smile. If a Hollywood special-effects department had been able tae reproduce that rictus grin it would have made several careers.

The Victim sat and sobbed at the TV, chain-smoking. The only thing she said to me was, – Any cigarettes, Lloyd . . . in a breathless, hoarse voice. Eventually they left and ah took the tupperware bowl down to Mrs McKenzie. Ah was heading through to Glasgow for the weekend to see some mates there. Ah was looking forward to it, fucked off as ah was wi Edinburgh. The thing was that ah had said tae ma mate Drewsy that I'd help him out the morn's morning which ah wisnae really up for but it wid be cash in hand and ah needed hireys for the weekend.

4

DREWSY AND ME are in this Gumleyland ghetto. Ah think it's Carrick Knowe but it could be Colinton Mains. Ah was fucked and hungover in the van. – It's just a skirtin job, Lloyd. That and new doors. Take nae time at aw, he telt ays.

Drewsy always seems to be smiling because he has laughing eyes and Coke-bottle glasses. The thing is that he is a very happy cunt and gives off a good vibe. Ah worked with him ages ago out at Livingston in a sweat-shop where we built house-panels, and since he went tae graft for himself he always puts a bit of casual my way if he can; which was champion the fuckin wonderhoarse fir the Double L. Oh. Y. D.

At the house, the boy, a Mr Moir, makes us a cup ay tea. – Anything you need, lads, just give's a shout. I'll be in the garden, he told us cheerfully.

Anywey, wir knockin oaf the rooms finestyle, and I'm starting tae feel better, looking ahead tae the night oot wi the Weedgie cunts. Drewsy and me are in this room which is like a young lassie's bedroom. There's a big poster ay the boy fae Oasis oan one waw, one ay the gadge fae Primal Scream and one fae the dude oot ay Blur oan the other. Close tae the bed, though, is the boy oot ay Take That, him that went and left. There's a few tapes thair n aw. Ah pit oan Blur's *Parklife*, cause ah quite like the title track where ye hear the boy that wis in *Quadrophenia* spraffin away. That wis a fuckin good film.

Ah start singing along as ah rip oot the old skirting-board.

– Hey! Phoah . . . look at this! Drewsy shouts. He's rummaging through the lassie's chest ay drawers and ah know which one he's looking for. He locates the underwear drawer pretty sharpish, pulling a pair ay panties oot and sniffing at the crotch. – Wish tae fuck ah could find the dirty laundry basket, he laughs, then, suddenly inspired, goes out into the hallway and opens a few presses. There's nothing there though – Bastard. Still, some nice wee panties here, eh?

– Fuckin hell, man, ah'm totally in love wi this wee chick, ah tell him, hudin up a pair ay scanties tae the light and trying to mentally visualise a nice fuckin hologram tae fit intae them. – How auld dae ye reckon she is?

– Ah'd say between fourteen and sixteen, Drewsy smiles.

– What a fuckin ice-cool wee bird, ah say, looking

through the spot-on-sexy collection of undies. I take out
Blur and put on Oasis who are giving it laldy and ah don't
really like bands being mair ay a club sort ay cunt but ah
decide that I'm up for this. Ah go back to my skirtings but
Drewsy's still intrigued.

Ah look up and jump as Drewsy's dancing around tae the
music, but he's goat a pair ay the lassie's knickers stretched
ower his heid and his glesses oan toap. At that point ah at
first think then I definitely know that I'm hearing something from outside and before ah can shout tae Drewsy the
door opens and it's the guy, Mr Moir, standing there, in
front of Drewsy who's dancing away. – What's going on!
What are you doing? That's . . . that's . . .

Poor Drewsy pulls the pants off his heid. – Eh, sorry,
Mr Moir . . . jist huvin a wee joke, eh. Ha ha ha, he says
adding a playful, stage laugh.

– Is that your idea of humour? Going through someone's personal belongings? Acting like an animal in my
daughter's underpants!

It was that bit that got me. Ah started laughing
uncontrollably. Ah had the Flight Lieutenant Biggles in a
big way. Ah was contorting like ah was having a fit and
ah could feel my face reddening. – Heagh heagh heagh
heagh . . .

– And what are you sniggering at? He turned to me,
– You think that's fuckin funny! This . . . fuckin sick
imbecile rummaging through my daughter's personal
items!

– Sorry ... Drewsy weakly lisped, before ah could speak.

– Sorry? Fuckin sorry are ye! Have you got children? Eh?

– Aye, ah've got two laddies, Drewsy said.

– And you think that's the way a father should behave?

– I've said I'm sorry. It was a stupid thing tae dae. We were just having a laugh. Now we can stand here and discuss how faithers should behave or me and my mate can get on and finish the job. Either way, you get billed. What's it to be?

Ah thought Drewsy was cool, but the cunt Moir didnae think so. – Take your tools and leave. I'll pay ye for the work that you've done. You should think yourself lucky you aren't getting reported!

We tidied up, the cunt coming back in and moaning at us occasionally, oblivious tae the fact that he was carrying his daughter's underpants around with him, clenched tightly in his hand.

Drewsy and me hit the pub. – Sorry ah couldnae tip ye oaf in time, Drewsy. It wis the music. Ah never heard the sneaky cunt. One minute nae sign, the next the cunt wis standin over ays watchin you daein yir wee dance.

– One ay they things, Lloyd, Drewsy smiled. – Good fuckin laugh though, eh. Did ye see the cunt's face?

– Did ye see yours?

– Right enough! he exploded with laughter.

DREWSY PEYED AYS and we drank up. Ah got a taxi up tae Haymarket and got oan the train tae Soapdodge City. When ah got off at Queen Street ah took a taxi up tae Stevo's flat in the West End, travelling the same distance as in the Edinburgh taxi but for about a third of the price. It reminded me what cunts Edinburgh taxi drivers were. Ah wis nearly fuckin well cleaned oot already. Ah would have tae try tae flog they shitey Es ay The Poison- ous Cunt's.

Claire, Amanda and Siffsy were at Stevo's and they were all getting togged up. – What the fuck's this fashion parade fir, man? ah bleated nervously, checking the in- adequacy ay ma ain togs.

– Wir no gaun tae The Sub Club now, cause Roger Sanchez is on at The Tunnel, Claire said.

– Fuckin hell . . . ah whinged.

– You're awright, Stevo said.

– Ye think so?

– Aw aye, Claire nodded.

Siffsy kept buttin in and oot ay the front room, treatin it like a fuckin catwalk. He wis takin ages. – Ah don't know about they shoes n strides wi this toap, eh said.

– Naw, ah said, – the strides dinnae really go wi the toap, eh no.

– Ah cannae no wear the toap though, man. Sixty-five bar oot ay X-ile. Thing is, if ah wear they broon strides they'll clash wi the shoes.

– We need tae go, said Claire rising, – c'moan.

Amanda and Stevo followed her lead. Ah couldnae get it together to stand up, it was a cracker ay a couch, you just sank doon intae it.

– Hud oan a minute! Siffsy begged.

– Get tae fuck, Stevo shook his head. – C'moan, Lloyd, ya fuckin east-coast poof. Ye fit?

– Aye, ah said, rising.

– Ah'll no be a minute . . . Siffsy pleaded.

– See ye in the next life, Stevo said, exiting, as we followed. Siffsy came behind feeling self-conscious about the Gordon Rae's.

HIS EMBARRASSMENT EVAPORATED at The Tunnel. They Es Stevo had got were shit-hot, much better than the crap I'd brought through if the truth be telt. Roger S was on fine form and we were well away with it when we headed back to Stevo's the next morning. Siffsy started tae get self-conscious again as the E ran down, and fucked off hame tae get changed. Ah dropped one of The Poisonous Cunt's 'business' acids back at the gaff on the proviso that if her eckies were shite then her acids wouldnae be too hot either.

Ah took out my plastic bag of Es from doon my baws. – These are shite, ah said holding them up to the light.

Ah'll never fuckin well sell these. Ah stuck them down on the table.

None of the poofy Weedgie cunts were into daein trips. Stevo stuck on the telly while Amanda and Claire started spliff-building.

The acid wasn't up to much at first. Then it kicked up. Then it kicked up some mair.

5

THERE IS A ringing in my ears and ah hear some cunt say something which sounds a little like 'perhaps they'll understand the truth someday of why things remain different' in an accent which is reminiscent of The Crow's: not quite Manc, a bit more small-town East Lancs.

Who said that? Ah start to panic because it's goat nae context and because nobody could have said it. There are four of us in the room: me, yes, I'm here, and there's Stevo, who is sitting watching the golf or rather watching the blue arse of this guy who may or may not be a golfer; Claire, lying on the couch laughing loudly and talking about why people in the catering game make crap shags (fatigue through unsocial hours and alcohol-induced impotence ah think she concluded – a bit unfairly, I'm thinking, but well, fuck it); and Amanda is here too, eating strawberries with me.

We're eating strawberries and cream cheese.

The best approach is to slice the strawberry, kind of

cross-sectioning it. This reveals an aspect of the fruit we seldom see. Aye right ye are, ya daft cunt. Then just enjoy the reverb of the red and white and watch the brown carpet in the room change into polished, speckled-marble floor tiles and extend luxuriously into infinity and doing this, just indulging the whim ah see myself moving away from Amanda and Claire on the couch and Stevo, who's still watching the golf and I'm screaming: PHOAHH YA CUNT THAT YE ARE FUCK THIS MAN and ah drop the strawberry and the room assumes something approximating its normal dimensions and they look round at me and Stevo puckers his lips which look like huge strawberries and Claire laughs even more loudly causing me to emit gasping, fractured, machine-gun laughter and now Amanda's at it too and I'm going: – All hands on deck! These are good fuckin trips, ah'm off ma fuckin tits here, man . . .

– You've got the Flight Lieutenants in a big way there, Lloyd, Stevo laughs.

It's true. Ah have.

To calm down ah start on the master-chef preparation for the strawberries which becomes something of an urgent mission in my head. This is not because I'm para or fuck all like that, but because there is a vacuum, a space in my head, which will be filled with bad thoughts if ah don't busy busy chop chop these strawbs and the trick is to daintily use this sharp knife to stab some cunt

Eh

All hands on deck! These are good fuckin trips, ah'm off ma fuckin tits here, man . . .

No no no fuck off the trick is to why did ah say that no no no bad thoughts cannae be explained, that makes them worse, they just have to be ignored because what you do with the knife is to remove the white bit of the strawberries and fill the resulting hole with cream cheese with a knob of cream cheese with the cream of knob cheese of what

Fuck

Ah don't know if I'm thinking this or saying it or both at the same time, but you can sometimes say one thing while thinking another. So if I'm saying this, actually saying this out loud, what am ah thinking? Eh? Ah ha!

– Listen, wis ah gaun oan aboot the strawberries, ah mean was ah talkin oot loud aboot it? ah ask.

– You were thinking out loud, Stevo says to me.

Thinking. That's what ah was doing, but wis ah thinkin out loud? Cunts are fuckin well trying to wind me up but it takes more than a wee tab ay LSD to knock auld Lloyd Buist here out of his fuckin stride ah will tell you that for nothing matey of the seven seas. – Thinking out loud, ah said or thought.

Ah said, because Claire says, – Drug psychosis, Lloyd, that's what it is. The first sign.

Ah just laugh and keep repeating: – Drug psychosis drug psychosis drug psychosis

– Fine by us you eatin aw the strawberries by the by, Lloyd, Amanda says.

Ah look at the punnet and sure tae fuck the remnants of strawberries are in evidence, husks n that, but examples of the fruit in its complete state are conspicuous by their absence. Greedy guts, Lloyd, I think to myself.

– Greedy guts Lloyd, Claire says.

– Fuckin hell, Claire, ah wis jist thinkin they words . . . it's like telepathy . . . or did ah say thum . . . this acid is fuckin really mad n the strawberries, ah've eaten aw the strawberries . . .

Ah start to panic a little bit. What's got me is that with the strawberries being consumed I've lost my means of space-and-time travel. The strawberries were my space craft/time machine; no that's too simple, too crass, delete that line of thought and start again: the strawberries were my means of transportation from this dimension or state into another. Without strawberries I'm condemned to live in their fucking world which is no good at all because without hallucinations of a visual and auditory nature, acid is pretty crap; ah mean you might as well just be pished out of your face beery and bleary, giving profits to the brewers and the Tory Party which you do everytime you raise a glass of that shite to your lips but without the hallucinations the only advantage you had with the old acceeeed was the Flight Lieutenants which is still better than bevvy because you just looked a moosey-faced cunt sitting drinking the depressant called alcohol so fuck that that was it for me it was STRAWBERRIES . . .

– Ah'm away doon tae the deli fir mair ay they straw-berries, eh, ah announced. Something in Claire's face made me laugh. Ah took a chronic attack of the Flight Lieutenants.

– You mind yirsel, trippin like that, Claire said.

– Aye, watch, Amanda nodded.

– Mad gaun oot like that, Stevo turned his attention from the golfer's blue arse.

– Naw man, it's sound, ah said. – Ah feel great.

Ah do. It's barry tae ken that people actually care about me. Not enough tae stop me fae gaun oot or to say 'I'll chum ye' but that just could be paranoia. Ah said ah wanted to be alone did I say

Ah wanted tae be

Ah do a pish before ah go. Ah hate pishing on acid because you never feel like you're finished and the distortion of time makes you think you've been pishing longer than you have and it gets boring and the next thing ah know is that I'm fed up with this pish and I'm putting my cock away before it's actually finished, well, it's *finished* but I've not really shaken it out but fuck me I'm no wearing jeans I'm wearing flannels it would not be so fuckin bad with denims but with flannels I'll have a map of South America or Africa on my groin unless ah take some positive fuckin action which ah do stuffing bog paper down my keks. My keks. Stuffing. Accusations fly. J'accuse. Fuck off. It's Lloyd Buist.

Lloyd Buist is my name, no Lloyd Beattie. B.U.I.S.T. Another bad attack of the Flight Lieutenants. Breathe easy . . .

Imagine getting me, Lloyd Buist, *me*, confused with Lloyd Beattie, the cunt that was rumoured to have shagged his wee sister. Ah huvnae even got a fuckin wee sister. I rest ma fuckin case, your honour; your judge, jury and executioner psychopath who begins every Leith pub conversation with: Ah mind ah you. You wir the dirty cunt that . . .

Ah mean, how the fuck can you get us mixed up? Yes, we both live in Leith, and are similar ages. Granted, our given name is Lloyd . . . indeed an uncommon name for Leith. Okay, myself and the other Lloyd both have the first initial B in our surnames. Oh, I suppose there is one other area of similarity, your honour; okay, it's time to come clean: we both shagged our sisters. What can I say? Keep it in the family. No waste of time with long chat-up lines and Bacardis. Just, hi sis, awright? Up for a shag? Eh? Aye? Sound. Well, in my case it was some other cunt's sister. Awright? Awright, ya cunts? The rock opera I'm composing about Lloyd Beattie, the other Lloyd:

> In his hometown, Lloyd sits and waits
> Lloyd masturbates
>
> From his bedroom window
> Lloyd looks down and out
> Lloyd looks out and down
> Aint nuthin out there but town.

That is fuckin shite cause it's too personal cause it's about me, or as ah was as a young teenager and this is supposed to be about Lloyd Beattie and ah have to try and understand the complexities which led Lloyd Beattie into this incestuous affair with his sister cause these things dinnae just fuckin happen, no just like that, but hud oan the now . . . if Lloyd B. Numero Uno whom ah must call The Non-Wee-Sister-Shagging Lloyd, i.e.: my good self, sat and wanked as a bored sexually repressed fourteen-year-old in his bedroom in Leith, what was Lloyd Numero Two doing; he who did, or was said to have, knobbed his junior femme sibling? Probably the same as Lloyd One, the same as aw Leith fourteen-year-aulds at the time. But he didnae jist wank the dirty cunt, he took it a stage further involving a wee lassie who was just twelve at the time they said, a mess for the social workers, relatively speaking . . .

But ah am fuck all like that freak, we share a name . . . that's aw . . . take it easy, it's this fuckin acid. Back through to my friends to say proper bye-byes before ah finally, for good, once and for all, head for the deli.

– Ah never shagged my wee sister, ah tell them back in the front room.

– You've no got a wee sister tae shag, Stevo says, – if you did you probably would have though.

Ah think about this. Then something queasy moves in my stomach. I've had fuck all to eat in a couple of days bar Ecstasy, amphetamine sulphate and acid. Ah had one

Lucozade Isotonic drink though, and a bit of a pear that Amanda had and of course, the cream cheese and the STRAWBERRIES. Time to go.

AH LEFT THE flat and bounced, yes bounced down the Great Western Road. Lloyd Buist, ah keep telling myself. It seemed important to remember. Leith. A party refugee. The most oppressed kind. Fight for the right to party; fuck diverting your energies into frivolous nonsense like food and jobs and the likes. Boring, boring fuckin boring. Party refugee Lloyd, stranded in Glasgow's West End. Ah was lost in France, in love. Naw naw ya daft cunt. You are just on a simple message. A simple fuckin message

– Awright, big man!

Two young guys are beside me, breathing heavily and looking around, not meeting my eyes as they swivel their heads. It's these boys . . . Robert and Richard, from that Maryhill posse. Ah keep running into these boys, at The Metro, The Forum, Rezurrection, The Pure, The Arches, The Sub Club . . . big Slam punters, naw Terry n Jason . . . Industria . . . – Awright, boys!

Their faces look distorted, and they are already moving away from me with great haste.

– Sorry, big man, cannae stoap, wi did a wee dine and dash . . . yuv goat tae fir fuck sake, know what ah mean, big man . . . ah mean ye cannae gie up the clubbin n that jist tae eat . . . Robert gasps out running backwards like a referee. That's a good skill.

– That's it, boys! That's fuckin right! Good skills, Roberto! Good skills, Roberto my son! Ah shout encouragingly as they bomb off down the road. Ah turn around and this huge juggernaut is bearing down on me and ah tense up ready cause this mad cunt is gaunnae swing for me, going to attack the innocent Lloyd of Leith displaced person unaccustomed to your Weedgie ways but naw he's off doon the road in hot pursuit of Richard and Robert who are heading towards the Underground at Kelvin Bridge and the bloated alcoholic will never capture the younger fitter men because their bodies are honed by dance and Ecstasy; these boys are as fit as fuck and the more weighty, beefy fellow (he's no that fat) realises this and gives up. Our heroes escape, leaving their breathless pursuer panting heavily with his hands on his hips.

I'm laughing. The boy's coming ower tae me but ah cannae stop. Flight Lieutenant Biggles is the name. – Where dae these cunts stey! he sort ay gasps and snaps. It's like Lloyd of Leith, a good boy, a decent, hardworking Edinburgh merchant-school lad who plays squash and loves nothing better than attending big rugby internationals at Murrayfield is being lumped alongside Ricardo and Roberto, two schemies from a Weedgie slum.

This is a bit like being accused of shagging the sister ah don't have.

– Eh? Ah think ah manage tae cough out.

– These cunts are your fuckin mates. Where dae they fuckin stay?

– Fuck off, ah say, turning away. Then ah feel his airm on my shooder. He's gaunnae hit ays. No. He's no gaunnae let ays go. That is worse. Violence in the form of blows ah can take, but the idea of being constrained, no fuckin way . . . ah punch him, in the chest, what a place to punch any cunt, but ah didnae want to really punch him, just get him tae let go, and that's nae good cause as any wideo will tell you, you either punch some cunt or you dinnae and silly wee halfway-house slaps and pushes just make you look a cunt so ah start *really* punching the boy but it feels like I'm punching a mattress and he's shouting: – Phone the polis! Phone the polis! This man's ran out of my restaurant without paying, and I'm screaming: – Lit go ya cunt it wisnae fuckin me, and punching at the cunt but ah feel like rubber and I'm out of breath and he keeps a grip, his face aw screwed up and determined through its fear and apprehension

and

and a polisman is beside us. He's pulled us apart.

– What's this? he asks.

Ah've got four trips in my flannels. My poakits. The wee poakit, the compartment. Ah feel them. The cunt is saying: – This guy's mates ran up a food and drinks bill for nearly a hundred and twenty pound and then did a runner! I'm fishing out those wee squares of impregnated paper.

– This true? the polisman turned tae me and asked.

– How the fuck dae ah ken, eh, ah mean, ah jist sees they two guys runnin doon the road. Ah recognised one ay them vaguely fae The Sub Club so ah jist lets ontae the boy. Then this cunt here, ah nods at the restaurateur, – he's eftir the two boys. Then he comes back and grabs a hud ay me.

The polisman turns back tae the restaurateur. Ah get the trips between my forefinger and thumb and ah swallow the lot, silly fuckin cunt; ah could have left them, the polis would never find them wouldnae search me anywey I've done nowt wrong but ah swallowed the fuckin lot when ah could've even fuckin flung them away. No thinkin straight . . .

They called the child Lloyd Beattie
the cunt grew up a right wee sweetie

Lloyd One calling Lloyd Two, can you hear me Lloyd Two? Can you hear me Lloyd Two? Can you hear

am I floating

The beefy bastard is not amused. – These cunts robbed me! Ah'm strugglin tae make this business pay n they fuckin wee toerags . . .

A few people had stopped to witness the commotion. Ah became aware of them for the first time when a woman whae'd been watchin us said: – You jist grabbed that laddie! Jist grabbed um! It wisnae anything tae dae wi the laddie . . .

– That's right, ah said, nodding at the cop.

– This true? asked the polisman.

– Aye, ah suppose, says the beefy restaurateur, looking aw fuckin sheepish as well he might because he tampered unjustly with one Lloyd Buist from Leith who is a waster and has set himself up in opposition to the fascist British state but who now to his extreme embarrassment finds one of its law enforcement officers taking his side and ticking off the capitalist businessman who tried to apprehend said Leith man.

Another woman says, – The likes ah you have goat enough bloody money as it is!

– That's fuckin men fir ye. Money, money, money, that's aw they think aboot, another one, the one that took my part, laughs.

– That n thir hole, the other woman said. Then she looks at the restaurateur and gives him a dismissive sneer.

The guy looks at her, but she's sort of staring him down and starts to say something then thinks better of it.

The cop rolls his eyes in a manner obviously meant to indicate exasperation but which seems a camp, theatrical gesture. – Look, says our lawman, looking bored, – we can play this by the rules which means I'll huv yis both doon the station n charged wi breach. He raises his eyebrows in a what's-it-to-be manner at the restaurateur who looks like he's shiting himself.

– Aw c'moan ... geez a brek, the restaurant guy appeals.

– You were out of order, pal, the cop lectures, pointing at the guy, – attempting to restrain this man when the culprits were in fact two other men. You admit that this man wasn't even in your restaurant?

– Aye, the guy said. He looks quite ashamed.

– Too right, ah goes. Cheeky bastard. Innocent passer-by me, eh, I said to the cop. He looks like Noddy.

He turns to address me, adopting that formal Officer-Of-The-Law mode, – And you, goes the polis, – you're out of your face. Ah dunno what the fuck you're on, and right now ah've goat far too much on tae be bothered. Any fuckin mair lip fae you and ah will be bothered. So shut it. He looks back to the restaurateur. – I want details from you, about the other two guys.

The guy makes a statement and gives the polis descriptions of the youths, as they say. Then we're made to shake hands, like we were bairns in a school playground. Ah think about taking exception to this patronising behaviour, but it feels strangely good to be magnanimous and ah can see the bruises and swelling coming up on the side of the poor cunt's face and ah was a bit out of order hitting the boy like that, poor cunt was upset at being ripped off and only trying tae get justice but wisnae thinking straight in his emotional state when he apprehended said Leith man. Then the lawman gets into his car and departs, leaving us looking at each other. The women have gone up the road.

– Embarrassment that, eh! The guy laughs.

Ah said fuck all; ah just shrugged at the cunt.

– Sorry, mate . . . ah mean, ye could've goat me intae bother thair. If ye'd pressed charges like. Ah appreciate it.

Get *him* intae fuckin bother . . . – Listen, ya daft bastard, ah wis trippin oot ay face n when that polis wanker came ah hud tae swallow some mair trips ah wis haudin. In aboot one minute ah'm gaunnae be totally cunted here!

– Fuck . . . acid . . . ah've no done acid for years . . . he said, then: – Listen, mate, come along the road wi me. Tae the restuarant. Sit doon for a bit.

– If ye goat drink thair, aye.

He nodded.

– Ye see the only thing ah can dae is have a good bevvy. It's the only way ye can control a trip: force doon as much alcohol as possible. It's a depressant, ken.

– Aye, awright. Ah've goat drink in the restaurant. I'd take ye for a beer in a boozer, but ah've goat tae get back and prepare for the night. Seturday night, the busiest time n that.

Ah'm in nae position tae refuse. The trips hit me like a slap in the face from a wet fish. Loads of wee explosions go off simultaneously in ma heid and ah realise that ah can see nothing at all, just a big golden light and some obscure

objects swirling around me out of reach. – Fuckin hell . . .
man, ah'm gaunnae die dinnae let ays walk intae that
road . . .

– S'awright, mate, ah've goat ye here . . .

The guy's holding me again, this time I'm keeping a
grip on him, even though he looks like that fuckin dinosaur in *Jurassic Park*, one ay they nippy wee cunts which,
awright, are wee by dinosaur standards, no as big as the
T. Rex; T. Rex, now there was a cunt: – Ah love to boogie
on a Saturday night . . . mind that cunt T. Rex?

– S'awright, mate, wir jist alang the road . . . wir jist
alang here . . . jist cause ah've goat a restaurant though,
pal, it disnae mean tae say that ah'm some big rich bastard
who's hud it aw handed tae them oan a silver plate. Ah'm
jist like they boys, they pals of yours. Stealin fae thir ain
kind! That's what that wis. That's the thing that disgusts
me the maist. Ah mean tae say, ah'm fae Yoker, ye know
Yoker? Ah'm a red sandstone boy, me.

He's fuckin rabbiting oan a load ay shite and I'm fuckin
blind and my breathing is fucked oh no don't think about
fuckin breathing no no no bad trip hopeless when ye
fuckin think aboot the breathing most bad trips happen
when you think about the breathing

but

but we're different from say dolphins, because these
daft cunts have tae think consciously about each breath

they take when they come up for air and that. Fuck that fir a game ay sodgirs the poor cunts.

No me but, no Lloyd Buist. A human with a superior breathing mechanism, safe from the acid. You didnae have to think aboot the breathing, it just happened. Yes!

What if

WHAT IF, BUT, no no no but what if no no no a staggering trip; me now flying off into space seeing the Buist body: a deserted shell being dragged along to the mass murderer pervert restaurateur's lair, this body being folded over a table with lubricants applied to the arsehole and penetration achieved just as the victim's carotid artery is severed with a kitchen knife. The blood is expertly drained off to be collected into a bucket to make black pudding and the body is systematically dismembered following being pumped with Yoker semen and that night in the trendy West End eating house the unsuspecting Weedgies sit spraffing unaware that instead of feasting on their usual dead rats they are munching the remains of Lloyd A. Buist, an unattractive divorcee of the parish of Leith, integrated into the City of Edinburgh in nineteen canteen, naw naw hud on, nineteen twenty cause ah ken my history and it's enough tae make yir hearts go ooh la la ah fancy a shag cause ah just saw something or someone gorgeous really fuckin gorgeous pass my line of trance-vision up here in the clouds but yeah, they took Leith into Edinburgh in spite of a popular plebiscite that rejected the merger by a ratio of something like seven billion to one but aye, they did it anyway because these stupid schemie cunts ken fuck all and they need a good benign central authority to tell them what is in their interest and that's how Leith has fuckin thrived ever since then ha ha ha like fuck . . . except for a few incoming yuppies but obviously the story of Leith had broader implications

– Ah've known hard times n aw, that's aw ah'm sayin, says my mate Red Sandstone Boy, as I snap back into my body with a shuddering jolt.

Ah still seem to be just breathing oot. There's nae sense of breathing in and if the breathing mechanism is part of the subconscious which it has to be, is that no precisely what the acid fucks up?

Precisely; Holmes. That means you are up shit creek, you daft cunt. – Ha ha ha ha ha ha ha ha ha ha ha ha ha ha ha ha ha ha ha ha ha ha ha ha ha ha ha ha ha ha ha ha ha ha ha ha ha ha ha ha ha Flight Lieutenant Biggles reporting for duty, sir. Biggles, old man, don't stand so bloody close to me and put away that weapon while I'm talking to you. Did ah tell ye that your breathing is rather laboured, it's aw fuck fuck fuck fuck

– Take it easy, mate, here we are.

No breathing.

No no no think of a Garden of Eden type scene where there are loads of sultry naked women lounging around and all of a sudden who should be here but Lloyd but the faces ah can't get the fuckin faces right n what if these cruel bastards in the research labs were to give dolphins LSD? I'll fuckin well bet it's been done before the cruel cunts. Amanda's showed me that stuff she gets stuff through the post that goes oan aboot what these cunts dae tae cats and dugs and mice and rabbits but that's nowt; that would be real cruelty: giein a dolphin LSD.

We are not now moving. Moving now not. Now we are not moving. We are somewhere else. Somewhere enclosed.
    – What's the fuckin score?
    – Take it easy there, yir hyperventilatin . . . I'll get ye a wee bevvy.
    – Whair the fuck is this?
    – Stay cool, mate, it's ma restaurant. Gringo's. Gringo's Mexican Cantina. Hodge Street. This is the kitchen.
    – Ah ken this place. Ah came here once. Barry cocktails. With ma then girlfriend. We drank cocktails. Ah love cocktails. Want one want one want one want one . . . oh excuse me, mate, ah'm fuckin trippin oot ay ma box here. PHOAH! Yuh cunt ye! Aye . . . my ex-girlfriend. Her name was Stella

and she was nice. We didnae love each other but, eh no, mate. It's nae good unless there's real love thair ken? Ye cannae settle for second best. What aboot the cocktails though, mate? Eh?

– S'okay pal. I'll make ye one. What is it ye want?

– A Long Island Iced Tea would be nice.

Nice. Ah keep saying that word, thinking that word. Nice.

So the boy starts mixin the cocktails and I'm in this kitchen and it's all flying away fae me but he's still going on about being a red sandstone boy who doesnae care aboot money . . .

– . . . a red sandstone boy. It's no that ah'm a money grabber and ah know that plenty people are starvin and homeless in Glasgow, bit that's the fuckin Government's fault, no mine. Ah'm tryin tae make a fuckin livin. Ah cannae feed aw the poor, this isnae a soup kitchen. Ye know how much they fuckin criminals at the council charge in rates for this place?

– Naw . . .

The boy should start a militant community group in Yoker and call it Red Sandstone. It sounds okay. Red Sandstone.

– It's no that ah'm a Tory, far fuckin from it, says Red. – Mind you, that council's jist a fuckin Tory council under another name; that's what that is. Is it the same in Edinburgh?

This is too fuckin radge. – Eh, aye, Edinburgh. Leith.

Lloyd. Ah nivir, ah mean, no the one that shagged ehs sister, that wis a different Lloyd . . . nice cocktail, mate . . .

A Long Island Iced Tea.

The cocktail is fuckin reverberating like anything. It's gaunnae explode . . .

– Cheers. Aye, see if ah wis votin fir any cunt, which ah'm no, ah'd vote SNP . . . naw, ah widnae, ah tell ye whae ah wid vote for if ah wis votin fir anybody now; mind that boy that got sent tae the jail for no peyin his poll tax?

This cocktail is the wrong one. Ah need a strawberry something, Strawberry, a Strawberry Daiquiri.

– What wis the boy's name?

– Strawberry Daiquiri.

– Naw . . . the boy that got sent tae the jail for no peyin his poll tax. The Militant boy.

Ah need strawberries . . . – A Strawberry Daiquiri, mate . . . that would dae me fine.

– Strawberry Daiquiri . . . aye, sure. Finish that Iced Tea first though, eh! Ah'll just have a wee beer this time, a San Miguel, naw, too heavy, maybe jist a Sol.

– Nae Becks, mate?

– Naw, jist Sol.

Red Sandstone gets up from the seat opposite me to fix the drinks and it's like a volcano exploding and fuck this, the roof is falling doon . . . not, ha ha ha fooled myself there, but the window has gone, that's fuckin defo.

– Sorry, ma man, nae strawberries. It'll huv tae be a Lime Daiquiri.

Nae fuckin strawberries . . . what a fuckin load ay shite, man . . . nae fuckin strawberries right enough the cunt goes so ah goes – Sound man, sound. And eh, thanks fir lookin eftir ays.

– Naw, ah sortay feel bad about it, you takin aw they trips n that. How ye feelin?

– Sound.

– Cause as ah say, ah'm jist tryin tae make a livin. But these guys, they're jist rubbish. They've goat the money tae go oot tae fuckin clubs aw night, but they steal food fae the likes of me. That's fuckin out of order.

– Naw, man, naw; ah admire they boys . . . they know that the game isnae fuckin straight. They know that there's a Government fill ay dull, boring bastards who gie the likes ay us fuck all and they expect ye tae be as miserable as they are. What they hate is when yir no, in spite ay aw thair fuckin efforts. What these cunts fail tae understand is that drug and club money is not a fuckin luxury. It's a fuckin essential.

– How can ye say that?

– Because we are social, collective fucking animals and we need to be together and have a good time. It's a basic state of being alive. A basic fuckin right. These Government cunts, because they're power junkies, they are just incapable of having a good fuckin time so they want everybody else tae feel guilty, tae stey in wee boxes and devote their worthless lives tae rearing the next generation of factory fodder or sodgers or dole moles for the state. It's these boys' duty as human fuckin beings tae go oot clubbin and partying wi their friends. Now, they need tae eat from time to time, it's obviously important, but it's less important than having a good fuckin time.

– Ye cannae admire people like that. That's jist rubbish, thon.

– Ah *do* admire the guys. Massive respect from Lloyd here; Leith's Lloyd, the one that never shagged his sister: massive respect tae they boys Richard and Robert fae Glesgie . . . dear auld Glesca toon . . .

– Thought you said ye didnae know them? Red Sand-stone's hurt face pouts out at me surrounded by a cacophony of clattering sounds and throbbing, pulsating lights . . .

– Ah know them as Richard and Robert; that's it, mate. I've blethered wi the boys, in chill-oot zones n that. That's as far as it goes . . . listen, ah'm fucked. Ah could be dying. Ah need tae get ma heid doon or something or another Sol . . .

The Sol and the Daiquiri and the Long Island Iced Tea are empty and ah cannae remember who drank them surely ah never ah mean

THE BOY GOES to make up some of the tables in the front dining area. Ah climb across the sink, through some dirty dishes and just slide like an eel out of the open window, falling onto some binliners stacked with rubbish and roll-ing into a dry drain in this concreted back court. Ah try tae stand up, but ah cannae, so ah just crawl towards this green gate. Ah just know ah have to go, to keep moving, but I've ripped my flannels and torn my knee and ah can see the flesh wound pulsating like an opened-up strawberry and now I'm on my feet which is strange because ah can't recall ever standing up and I'm on a busy main road which is maybe the Great Western or maybe Byre's or maybe Dumbarton and I can't see where I'm going and it should be home but that cannae surely tae fuck that cannae mean Stevo's flat.

The sun rises up above the tenements. I'm just gaunnae fly intae it.

Ah shout tae some people in the street, two lassies. Ah tell them, – The sun, I'm just up for flyin right intae it.

They say nothing, and they don't even notice as ah fly right up out of this world and its trivial, banal oppressions, right into that big fuckin golden bastard in the sky.

6

IT TOOK AYS a while tae get back fae Soapdodge City. Acid, man, fuck that, never again, never until the next time at any rate. When ah get back, The Poisonous Cunt's coming oot ay ma stair. – Where have you been? she says accusingly. The Poisonous Cunt is getting too fuckin possessive taewards me.

– Glasgow, ah tell her.

– What for? she asks.

– Slam night on the Renfrew Ferry, eh, ah lie. Ah don't want The Poisonous Cunt knowing my MO . . .

– What was it like?

– Awright, aye, ah goes.

– Ah've got some mair ay they Doves for you to punt, but they're back at mines, she says.

Great. Mair crap Es tae sell. Ma reputation will soon be so bad that people'll rather buy their chemicals fae Scottish and Newcastle Breweries. Ah left the other ones in

Glasgow wi Stevo, who wasnae too hopeful, but who said
that he would see what he could do.

– Right. Ah'll come up the night, ah tell her. Ah just
want to get in and make myself a cup of tea and a spliff.
Then ah realise that I've left my blow in Soapdodge City,
with those Es. – Have you got any blow? Ah need a fucking
blow. Ah'm exhausted after that trip. My jaw feels like it's
been broken. Ah need tae mellow out. Even some fuckin
jellies wid dae ays. Ah need some thing. Ah need, full
fuckin stop.

– Aye. Ah've got black and soapbar, she says.

– Right then, I'll chum you back to yours.

We get up to The Poisonous Cunt's and Solo is in, as well
as a couple of mates called Monts and Jasco. Ah was embarrassed as Solo started talking tae ays. Ah couldnae make
oot a word ay it. It sounded like he was forcing his syllables
out slowly through his nose. As The Poisonous Cunt went
to the kitchen to stick on the kettle and get some blow,
Monts stood behind Solo with a smirk on his face and
pushed out one cheek with his tongue, in the cocksucker
gesture. He and Jasco were like nothing more than two vul-
tures circling over a large wounded animal. Ah found it sad,
and ah felt sorry for Solo. It reminded ays ay a piece ay film
ay Muhummad Ali ah'd seen oan telly, stricken from his
articulate buoyancy by Parkinson's, probably brought on by
the fight game. The Poisonous Cunt, when she came in,
reminded me of Don King, manipulation screaming
through a smile of searing delight.

– You gaunnae take that gear doon tae Abdab for ays then? she enquired.

– Aye, ah told her. Abdab was an old mate ay mine down in Newcastle. The Poisonous Cunt was sorting him out with some shite and ah was delivering. It was a Paddy Crerand ah didnae feel like running. Ah only agreed to do it to see Abdab and his Geordie mates and have a night oot doon thair. Ah always liked Newcastle. Geordies are just Scots who can't blame the English for them being fucked up, the poor cunts.

Jasco starts giein ays a hard time. Ehs normally a cool cunt but ehs been a bit nippy lately. Too much freebasin gaun oan wi the cunt. – Listen, Lloyd, if ah've goat a heid-ache ah'll take some paracetamol.

– Eh? ah goes.

– And if ah've goat a bad stomach ah'll take some bicarb soda.

Ah'm a wee bit too slow oan the uptake the day tae suss oot the cunt's game.

– Git oaf ehs case, Jasco ya cunt, Monts sais.

– Naw, listen, Jasco continued, – the point is, ah didnae huv a heidache or a sair stomach the other night. Naw. What ah wanted was tae git oaf my tits oan Ecstasy. So why did this cunt sell ays paracetamol and bicarb? He pointed at me.

– Moan tae fuck, Jasco, ah said defensively, – they wirnae brilliant Es, granted, and ah telt ye that fae the off, but they wirnae *that* shite. I kept it light cause it was like

Jasco was in the mood where he couldnae decide whether or no he was bein serious or havin a jokey wee wind-up.

– Did fuck all fir me, man, he moaned.

– Hundred and twenty milligrams ay MDMA in them, the boy telt me, The Poisonous Cunt said.

That was bullshit. You were lucky if there was fifty mills in those Doves. You had to neck them two at a time for any buzz at aw.

– Aye, right, Jasco said.

– Fuckin wis. Rinty got them fae Holland, The Poisonous Cunt maintained. It was cool, her getting involved, because it stopped Jasco nippin at me.

– In ays fuckin dreams the cunt did. Scottish fitba clubs have spent longer in Europe than any pills youse cunts have been puntin, he grumbled at her.

Ah knew that the conversation would go on and on like this aw night and ah shot the craw as soon as it was possible. When ah got oot intae the street, ah saw this boy and bird gaun doon the road thegither, obviously really intae each other, no oan drugs or nowt. Ah thought, when wis the last time ah wis ever like that wi a lassie, withoot bein aw eckied up? In a fuckin previous life, that's when. Ah kicked a stane and it bounced up and rattled, but didnae brek, the windscreen ay a parked car.

7

Ah'd had a good one wi Abdab doon in Newcastle, but
ah wis fucked. He'd gied ays mair than a few grams ay
coke for The Poisonous Cunt and the packet burned a hole
in ma poakit oan the bus up. It was come-doon para stuff
but ah kept thinking aboot Nukes and half expecting the
DS tae come oan the bus at every stoap. It didnae happen.
Ah goat hame and made some soup.

Later on that night ah went up tae Tribal wi Ally. Ah
was just wanting tae crash but the cunt insisted that ah
came along. Ah even had tae take a couple of my ain Es
which was bad news. This batch were different again, like
Ketamine or something. Ah was pure cunted, ah couldnae
dance. Ah sat in chill-out and Ally spraffed with me.
– How you feelin, Lloyd?

– Fucked, ah sais.

– You should try some ay that crystal meth ah've got back
at the hoose. Didnae even fuckin well blink eftir ah'd snorted
that. Ah hud a fuckin hard-on man for three days, eh. Ah wis

gaunnae abandon this quest fir love n brek ma vows and bell Amber tae come roond n sit oan ma face. Didnae want tae fuck wi her heid even mair man though, eh.

– She in the night?

– Aye, she's upstairs. Her and that Hazel and Jasco. Jasco's been knobbin that Hazel, he observed with rueful bitterness, blowing air out through his teeth and pushing his hair back, – Ah might have tae move in thair masel, man.

Amber didnae take long to locate me. She relieved Ally, letting him have a spell upstairs on the floor. – Ye dinnae huv tae sit wi ays, ah slurred. – ah'm awright. Jist a bit cunted . . .

– Sawright, she snapped, holding my hand in hers, before thoughtfully adding, – aw aye, that Veronica wis lookin for you.

As usual, it took ays a second or two to work out who she meant, then it hit me. Veronica was the tasteless nickname some people occasionally gave tae The Poisonous Cunt.

– Is she in here the night? ah asked with some apprehension, checking Amber's watch tae see if we could make the curfew at Sublime or Sativa if it was a yes.

– Naw, this wis earlier at the City Cafe, eh.

Thank fuck. Ah took another pill and Ally, Amber and this young guy called Colin came back tae mine. Ah tried a shift oan the decks but ah was too fucked tae dae anything. This gig would be comin up soon n aw. We hud tae turn it doon cause the yuppie scum acroas the landin whae shouldnae be in Leith in the first place complained aboot the noise and ah didnae want the polis roond eftir what was gaun oan wi Nukes. It was a bit embarrassing as Amber was trying tae get intae Ally and this young Colin cunt was trying tae get intae her. If ah had a wee bit mair sexual ambivalence and energy, ah'd have tried to get intae the young guy just tae wind every cunt up even mair. Eventually, he went, then Ally did too and ah wanted Amber tae but she sat up all night playing music. Ah was cunted, ah telt her that ah was fir crashin. When ah woke up in the morning she was at the other end ay the bed, her feet in my face.

– How you doin, Lloyd? Amber asked.

She was pulling her trousers on, looking dead young with her make-up faded and ah was feeling a bit like some paedophile cunt, aye right ye are ya dirty wee fuckin stoat-the-baw cunt that ye are.

– Fine, ah goes.

– Dinnae look fine tae me. Your feet are boggin, by the way.

– It's good ay ye tae say so. That's real mates for ye. Ye want a coffee?

– Aye … sound. Dinnae go aw huffy but, eh, Lloyd. Everybody's feet smell eftir a night ay kickin it in trainers.

– Ah ken that. Take yours for instance. Fuckin mingin, they wir, ah say, rising to make the coffee, as she gies ays a long, contemptuous scowl.

Ah was feeling pretty ropey. The coffee wisnae daein it

for me. Ah had tae see The Poisonous Cunt. Ah hud no tae see The Poisonous Cunt. This was getting oot ay hand. Ally had left some ay that crystal meth and ah was intae giein it a go. Ah needed a hit ay something before gaun tae that place. – Ye want a snort ay this? ah asked Amber.

– Nup, widnae touch it.

– That's sensible, ah said, chopping up a couple of lines.

– You're mental, Lloyd. What dae ye dae that fir?

– Dinnae ken. There's something missing in ma life. Ah'm an auld cunt now, compared tae you at any rate, and I've never really been in love. That's fuckin sad, ah telt her, snortin the lines. They are rough and fiery as fuck on my nasal lining.

Amber said, – Aw Lloyd . . . and gave me a hug and ah wished that ah could be in love with her but I'm no, so nae sense in kiddin oan aye cause that's shite fir every cunt and aw yi'll get is a ride oot ay it and a ride is never worth a good friendship.

She left just as my head blew apart.

8

ALLY WAS RIGHT about this stuff. It was true: ye dinnae even blink for days. Ah was soon surging with energy and thoughts. Ah couldnae blink. Ah tried, tried tae force a blink as ah sat oan the lavvy daein a shite. Then something happened: ah couldnae stop blinking. Ah felt sick and thought ah was gaunnae pass out. Ah hit the cold lino on the bathroom floor and felt better with my red throbbing face against it. The blinking stopped and ah was alert again.

The door went and it was a guy called Seeker. He stepped past me into the hallway. He held up a bag and then hooked it onto a small, metal set of scales he'd produced. – Ten grams, he said, – take a dab.

Ah did, though ah couldnae really tell the purity ay the coke from it, cause I'm no a big coke-heid, although it seemed better than Abdab's. Ah asked Seeker if ah could snort a line. He rolled his eyes impatiently, then he chopped out one each for us on the worktop in my kitchen. Ah felt that satisfying numbness but ah was so up on the meth that a poofy line ay toot would make nae real difference. That whole fuckin bag would make nae difference. Anyway, ah gave Seeker his dosh and he fucked off. He's a weird cunt that, no intae any scene, but every cunt kens him.

Ah hive aboot a fifth ay the gear and stick in an equivalent ay non-perfumed talc and mix it. Thir isnae much ay a difference.

In the hoose ah couldnae settle. Ah wis phonin every cunt up and spraffin shite. Ah hud a red phone bill n nae dosh tae pey it, so ah always just go for it at times like that. Ah kept thinking about how ah got involved with The Poisonous Cunt. It was a while back, basically for reasons of finance. I'd do deliveries for her and Solo, who was like her boyfriend or husband or something like that. Solo was a radge, but since he'd received that bad kicking from this other firm he had never been such a potent force. He seemed slow, like sort of brain-damaged, after he was blootered unconscious. As Jasco once put it: – They ambulance radges that scraped Solo oaf the pavement seem tae huv left a wee bit ay the perr cunt behind.

Ah must admit that ah wasnae particularly heartbroken, but while he was a bad bastard, ye eywis kent where ye stood wi Solo. The Poisonous Cunt was a different matter. Ah should have suspected the worst when ah belled her and she wouldnae come to the phone. The Victim telt me that ah 'wis tae come round'.

When ah got there the front room was mobbed out. In a corner The Victim sat quietly, looking out the window,

her large black eyes tense and furtive, as if trying to antici-
pate fae where the next shattering blow was going to come
into her life. Bobby was there, displaying a smile that
dripped sinister contempt. Monts was there, totally
wasted, too wasted to even speak to me, while ah picked
out Paul Somerville, Spud Murphy and some other cunt
ah vaguely recognised. Solo sat in his wheelchair in the
corner. It was a fuckin hammer house ay horrors right
enough.

– The Poisonous Cunt got off her tits last night, Bobby
informed me. – Freebasing coke. She's oan a brutal bastard of a comedown. Ah dinnae envy ye, Lloyd.

Ah didnae need this shite. Ah was just here tae dae a bit
ay delivering. Ah went through to The Poisonous Cunt's
bedroom, tapping on the door first, and hearing a throaty
rasp which might have been come or fuck off, but ah
entered anyway.

The Poisonous Cunt was lying on her bed wearing a
garish red tracksuit. The telly was on a table at the bottom
of the bed. She was smoking hash. Her face was drained of
colour, but her black hair looked well washed, had a kind
of sheen to it. Her face, though, looked rough, scabby and
dehydrated and its contrast with the health of her hair
made her look like an old hag wearing a wig. She still had
her most startling feature ah had long admired, her thick
black eyebrows which joined in the middle, making her
look like one of those type of Celtic fans who always look
like Paul McStay. Under these brows she had narrow

green eyes which were permanently in shadow and usually half shut. Ah remember once when ah was eckied ah got an erection when ah saw her unshaved armpits visible in a white, sleeveless cotton top. Ah once had a wank about fucking her armpits, ah don't know why this should be, but sexuality's a weird cunt tae try and fathom oot. It caused me some angst for a while, well aboot two or three minutes. There was one particular time when ah was tripping in the chip shop at the Fit ay the Walk, unable to speak, unable to indicate what ah wanted, unable to think about anything but The Poisonous Cunt's armpits. It was Ally who had started me off about them. He was on acid at Glastonbury and he said in a posh voice: – That lashie Veronica: an awfay abundance ay hair that lashie . . . After that we couldn't keep our eyes off The Poisonous Cunt's armpits.

Her face twisted at me in ugly recognition, then into a cartoon of disapproval, and ah understood just then why it should really be totally impossible to fancy her.

The Poisonous Cunt shagging: what a thought right enough.

– Well? she snapped.

– Goat it likes, ah said, handing over the bag ay coke.

She tore into it like a predator having a frenzied feast, chopping and snorting, her face contorted the same way it was when ah once saw her rummaging for fag dowts in the contents of my rubbish bin, which she'd tipped out onto the newspaper when she'd run out of snout. Ah cursed her angrily that time, and she went timid as she rolled up a single skin of stale baccy.

It was the first and last time ah saw The Poisonous Cunt deferential.

It was Monts that had given her her nickname. He'd fucked her once and either wouldn't do again, or did do it but no tae her satisfaction, so she'd got the pre-vegetative Solo tae trash his coupon. – That Poisonous Cunt Veronica, he'd muttered bitterly when ah went to visit him in the hospital, his face wrapped in bandages.

– How ye feelin? ah asked. Ah was staring at her profile. Ah could see the ring in her navel where the top part ay her tracksuit had ridden up.

– Shite, she hissed, sucking on the cigarette.

– Dae some rocks, eh?

– Aye . . . she said, then she turned towards me, – ah'm feelin fuckin crap. Ah've goat bad PMT. The only thing that helps me whin ah'm like this is a good fuck. Ah willnae git one fae that fuckin cabbage through thair. That's aw ah want. A good fuck.

Ah realised that ah was looking straight into her eyes, then ah was tugging at her tracksuit bottoms. – Ah'm fuckin well up fir that . . .

– Lloyd! she laughed, helping me undress her.

Ah stuck my finger in The Poisonous Cunt's fanny, and it was dripping. She must've been touching herself or it was maybe the crack or something. Anyway, ah got on top of her and pushed my erection into her fanny. Ah was licking her craggy face like a demented dug wi a dry, chipped auld bone as ah pumped mechanically, enjoying her gasps and groans. She was biting my neck and shoulders, but the crystal meth had numbed my body and made it as stiff as a board and ah could have pumped all day. The Poisonous Cunt had orgasm after orgasm and ah showed nae signs ay coming. Ah stuck the poppers under her nose the final time and pushed my finger up her arsehole and she screamed like a fuckin banshee and ah expected everybody tae come ben the bedroom but nae cunt did. Ma heart was thrashing and ah was frightened ah'd just peg oot cause ah got that rapid blinking for a bit but ah managed tae control it. – That's it . . . that's enough . . . ah heard The Poisonous Cunt gasp as ah pulled out as stiff and tense as when ah had gone in.

Ah sat up on the bed trying to bend my stiff cock into a semi-comfy position in my jeans. It was like having a piece of wood or metal down your pants. You just wanted tae break it off and chuck it away. Ah shuddered at the thought of how high my blood pressure must be.

– That was fuckin mad . . . The Poisonous Cunt lay back and gasped.

Ah had tae lie with her until ah could hear the others go. Fortunately she fell into a deep sleep. Ah lay rigid, looking up at the ceiling and thinking aboot what the fuck ah was daein wi ma life. Ah reflected that ah should've fucked The Poisonous Cunt's airmpits while ah hud the chance. If ye huv tae dae something unsavoury that yir gaunnae regret as soon as you've done it, then at least realising a sexual fantasy would make it mair acceptable.

Eftir a bit ah went through tae the front room and noted that Solo and Jasco were asleep oan the couch. Ah left and wandered for a while through the city, ecky heads going to and coming from clubs smiling, arm in arm; pish-faces staggering down the road groaning songs and other cunts cocktailed oan aw sorts ay drugs.

9

Ally isnae amused and Woodsy's the source of his
irritation. – That cunt, man, thinks eh kin jist swan in
here like the pre-heart-attack Graeme Souness oan high-
grade cocaine spoutin the contents ay *Mixmag* like we
used tae dae wi the *NME* when we were younger, and
every cunt's meant tae say: Wow Woodsy, man, right on,
ya cunt, wow man, and queue up tae suck oan his cheesy
wee helmet. That. Will. Be. Fuckin. Right.

– He's bad enough now, wait till ye see the cunt once he
actually gets his hole, Monts smirked.

– Thankfully, there isnae much chance ay that, man,
Ally smiles, – that's what it's aboot, man, this arrogance. It's
just defiance. He's no hud his fuckin hole in yonks. That
fucks up any cunt's self-esteem. This ego-projection, man,
is just the cunt's wey ay copin. Once he gets his hole, he'll
actually calm doon. That's what aw this religion shite's
aboot.

– Well ah hope eh does. Either that or ah hope he just

gits so fuckin arrogant that he willnae even talk tae the likes ay us. Then it would be problem solved, Monts decides.

– Ah'd get a whip-round, man, thegither n pey fir a hoor tae dae the business oan the cunt, if it helped tae sort his heid oot, Ally said.

– Woodsy's awright, ah said. Ah was daein a gig wi him the morn so that obliged ays tae back the cunt up. – Ah mean, ah dinnae mind aw the referencing ay DJs n clubs aw the time. That's cool, save me buying *Mixmag* and *DJ* hearin that cunt recitin it tae ye. It's the religion shite ah cannae really git tae grips wi. Tell ye what though, man, ah respect the cunt for it.

– Fuck off, Lloyd, Ally says dismissively.

– Naw, ah thought it was a fad. Then ah read that book by that cunt that writes aboot E whae wis sayin that he kens monks and rabbis that take it tae get in touch wi thir spirituality.

– Lick on, dug's baws, Ally grins, – so man, you're tryin tae tell ays that eh talked tae God at Rezurrection?

– Naw, what ah'm sayin is that the cunt thinks eh does, and eh thinks it in good faith. So for him it's the same as it huvin happened. Personally ah jist think that he wis pure cunted and went intae the auld white room and had a hallucination, but he thinks it wis mair thin that. Neither ay us kin prove the other cunt wrong so ah huv tae accept that what the cunt says is real *fir him*.

– Shite. By that fuckin logic, man, some community-care cunt could tell ye he believes that he's fuckin Hitler or Napoleon, and you believe that?

– Naw . . . ah say, – it's no a question ay *believin* some cunt's reality as they see it, it's a question ay *respectin* some cunt's reality as they see it. Of course, that's as long as they dinnae hurt any other cunt.

– Declare a fuckin interest here but, Lloyd ya cunt: you're jist backin the cunt cause ay the gig yir daein fir the guy, man. The Rectangle. Pilton. A Tuesday eftirnoon! It'll be pony, Ally laughs.

– Sounds a wee bit dodgy right enough but, Lloyd, Monts laughs.

This bullshit is getting ays well nervy and hyper aboot this fuckin gig.

10

JUST TALKING ABOOT Woodsy got me nervous about the gig. The mair ah thought aboot it, the mair uncool it was. Woodsy was planning to have a rave at the Rectangle Club in Pilton (or Reck-Tangle as he'd put on the flyers) on a Tuesday afternoon. That was pretty fuckin weird in itself. Ah tried to get every cunt to come, but Ally said no way, just because of how he felt about Woodsy.

Amber and Nukes were up for it but, and Drewsy ran us down in the van. When we got there nae cunt was around except the hall caretaker. Woodsy already had his decks, mixer, amps and speakers set up. His gear was better than Shaun's so I wanted a shot before I started.

Woodsy came in a wee bit later with this minister cunt. – This is Reverend Brian McCarthy of East Pilton Parish Church. He's supporting the gig, Woodsy telt us. This straight-peg cunt in a dog-collar grins at us. Ah wondered if he was eckied.

Ah didnae huv long tae wait before findin oot cause

Woodsy goes, – Ah've goat some fuckin good Es here, and handing one over to the Rev., urged him, – Neck it, Bri.

– I'm afraid I can't take . . . *drugs* . . . the poor cunt sais, looking horrified.

– Neck it, man, neck it and find the Lord, says Woodsy.

– Mr Woods, I can't condone drug-taking in my parish . . .

– Aye, well, whaire's aw yir parishioners then, eh? Woodsy growled, – Yir church wisnae exactly stowed oot when ah wis doon last Sunday. Mine wis!

There were some wee kids and some mothers and toddlers coming into the hall. – When's this rave startin then? a woman asked.

– In a wee minute, eh, Amber told her.

– It's great thit thir daein this for the bairns, another mother said.

The minister cunt walked away, leaving Woodsy shouting at him: – Fuckin hypocrite! You've nae spirituality! Dinnae fuckin tell ays otherwise! Satanic cunt in a cloth! Thirs nae church except the church ay the self! Thirs nae medium between man and god except MDMA! Fuckin scam artist!

– Shut it, Woodsy, ah sais, – c'moan, let's git started. A crowd were clocking the embarrassed minister leaving.

There were plenty young cunts coming in. – They should aw be at school, Amber went.

When ah got in ah'd noted that two hard bastards had got a table-tennis table out and had started playing in the middle ay the dance floor. Woodsy flipped when he saw them. – Hi! We've booked this! he snapped.

– You wantin a fuckin burst mooth, ya cunt? You're no fae here! one of the nutters snarled.

– The boy's right, Woodsy, this isnae your club, ah cut in, – thirs plenty room here. Youse dinnae mind us playin our sounds and huvin a bop, boys? Ah addressed this remark tae the hardest-lookin ay the two hard cunts.

– Dae whit yis like, eh, the probably hardest cunt replies.

Ah got up and started puttin on the tunes. At first ah wisnae really mixin, just sort ay playing the sounds like, but then ah started really gaun for it, tryin oot one or two things. It was shite, but ah was so intae it, every cunt was getting intae it tae. The mothers n toddlers were jumpin, the wee neds were rave-dancing wi each other and even the two hard cunts had stopped playin the t.t. and were going fir it. Woodsy's Es were all snapped up and Amber even managed to flog a few ay ma Doves. Ah necked a couple myself and swallowed a wee wrap ay that crystal meth. Within an hour, the place was fill tae the brim. At first ah didnae see the polis come in, but the guy pulled the plug oan us and broke it up, before perr auld Woodsy got a chance to dae anything.

Then ah went up to the toon tae this club that wis oan and then ah saw her.

11

You CAN TELL that something's cooking in the emotional stratosphere beyond the buzzes ay the drugs U4E when your personal behaviour starts to change. Since ah met her last week ah've started to shower every day and brush my teeth twice a day. Ah've also taken to wearing fresh pants and socks on a daily basis which is a killer at the launderette. Usually one pair ay Ys lasted during the week and the other pair did for the clubbing. Most crucially, ah've been scrubbing under the helmet meticulously. Even the flat looks different. No clean and tidy exactly, but better.

Nukes is up for a blaw. It's strange that Nukes is such a peaceable guy who would never think of ever getting intae bother outside the fitba. Saturday though, it's all different: a different Nukes comes out to play. But no now. He's taken a back seat oan everything since the polis clocked him. I'm a wee bit stoned. I'm really better talking tae Ally aboot affairs ay the heart, but Nukes is pretty cool.

– See, Nukes, ah'm no used tae this game, eh no? Ah mean ah've nivir really been in love before so ah dinnae ken whether or no it's real love, the chemicals or just some kind ay infatuation. There seems tae be something thair though, man, something deep, something spiritual . . .

– Cowped it yit? Nukes asks.

– Naw naw listen the now . . . sex isnae the issue here. We're talkin aboot love. Electricity, chemistry n aw that – but beyond that, cause that's sex, just the buzz. But ah dinnae ken what love is, man, likesay *being in love*.

– You wir mairried wir ye no?

– Aye, donkey's years ago, but ah didnae have a clue then. Ah wis only seventeen. Aw ah wanted was ma hole every night, that wis the reason tae git mairried.

– Good enough reason. Nowt wrong wi yir hole every night, eh.

– Aye, aw right, but ah soon discovered that, aye, sure, ah wanted it every night awright, but no offay the same lassie. That wis when the trouble started.

– Well that's mibbee it but, Lloyd. Mibbee you've jist found the definition ay true love: Love is when ye want yir hole every night, but offay the same lassie. There ye go. So did ye git yir hole offay this bird then?

– Listen, Nukes, thir's some lassies that ye git yir hole offay, and there's others that ye make love tae. Ken what ah mean?

– Ah ken that, ah ken that. Ah fuckin well make love tae

them aw, ya cunt, ah just use the expression 'git yir hole' cause it's shorthand and sounds a bit less poofy, eh. So where did ye meet this bird?

– Up The Pure, eh. It wis her first time there.

– It's no a stoat-the-baw job, is it? That's your usual fuckin style, ya cunt!

– Like fuck, man, she's aboot twenty-six or some shite. She wis mairried tae this straight-peg, n she just fucked off and left him. She was oot wi her pal, jist her first or second time eckied like.

Nukes pits his hands up in front ay his face. – Whoah . . . slow doon thair gadgie . . . what ye fuckin well saying tae ays here? Ye meet this bird whae's oot fir the first time since she escaped this straight-peg, she's taken her first ever ecky, you're E'd up and yir talkin love? Sounds a wee bit like the chemical love tae me. Nowt wrong wi that, but see if it lasts the comedoon before ye start thinkin aboot churches, limos and receptions.

– Well, we'll see, ah say tae Nukes, noticing how different each ay his profiles is. One side ay his face is dead handsome, the other really geekish. The American-evening-television Nukes and the American-daytime-television Nukes. I'm tryin tae visualise Heather in her totality. All I can think about is eyes and face. It strikes me that ah dinnae even ken what her tits and arse are like: size, shape, form n aw that. It surprises me; ah always clock that sort ay thing first. My face seems never tae be more than a few feet fae hers when we're thegither. This is defo different, but it would be fuckin horrible tae die the now, just fuckin peg oot withoot ever huvin that total sense ay her.

– Tread warily, Lloyd, that's aw ah'm sayin, Nukes turns tae show off his good side, – Ye ken how easy it can be tae feel great aboot somebody when yir eckied up. Ah mind ay once a few ay us gaun through tae a Slam do oan the Renfrew Ferry. Ah wis jist comin up oan ma pill n Henzo comes runnin up tae ays sayin, fuckin battle stations here, ye cunt, the place is full ay Motherwell cashies. So ah looks over and sure enough, it's the whole Saturday Service crew, top boys n aw, groovin doon in a big wey. So ah turns tae Henzo an says: just fuckin chill ya tube. Every cunt's fuckin loved-up the night. They boys are sound. They're jist like us, eh; they'll take the fuckin buzz where they can find it. Disnae matter whether it's the house buzz wi the E or the swedge buzz wi the adrenalin, it's aw the same. So ah goes up tae this big cunt ah recognised and wi jist point at each other and laugh for a bit, then it's big hugs aw roond. He introduces ays tae the rest ay his crew and we're pertyin away thegither. He says tae me: this rush isnae quite as good as the swedge rush, but ye can get tae sleep easier eftir a few nights. Ah'm up fir days wi the swedge rush, cannae sleep or fuck all. That's us big mates, but jist wait till we're next at Fir Park. Nae quarter asked or given, eh.

– So what ye sayin?

– It's like at a rave we create a kind ay environment, and it isnae just the E – although it's maistly the E – that encourages that kind ay feelin. It's the whole vibe. But it doesnae transfer that well tae the ootside world. Oot thair, these cunts have created a different environment and that kind ay environment lends itself mair tae the swedge rush.

– Thing is but, ye could still find love, real love, in the club environment. It just helps people tae get thegither, tae open up mair and lose thir inhibitions. Nowt wrong wi that.

– Ah bit listen tae this. Sometimes the whole thing plays tricks oan ye. When yir eckied, every bird looks a fuckin doll. Ye want tae try the acid test: go oot wi her trippin the next day. See what she looks like then! Ah remember one night at Yip Yap ah pills this wee bird. Fuckin tidy n aw, ah'm telling ye, man. So the emotions are sizzlin away and bein a romantic type ay cunt ah suggests a wee walk up Arthur's Seat tae watch the sun comin up, eh no?

– Bein E'd up oot yir face, ye mean.

– That's exactly the fuckin point but! If ah wis jist left tae ma ain devices ah wid huv said somethin like: fancy comin back tae ma place, ken? Bit naw, cause ah wis eckied ah acted in a different wey fae usual. Mind you, the thing is that now ah'm eywis eckied so that's become the fuckin normal wey ah do act! But anywey, what wis ah sayin?

– The bird, Arthur's Seat, ah reminds him.

– Aye, right . . . well, this bird thinks, cause she's E'd in aw, she's thinkin tae herself: this is a romantic cunt. So wir up oan Arthur's Seat and ah looks at her in the eye and

Thing is but, ye could still find love, real love, in the club environment. It just helps people tae get thegither, tae open up mair and lose thir inhibitions. Nowt wrong wi that.

says: ah really want tae make love tae ye now. She's up for it, so it's oaf wi the fuckin gear n we starts gaun for it, cowpin away, looking doon oan the city, fuckin great it wis. Thing is, about ten minutes intae it, ah started tae fell like shite. Ah goat aw that creepy, tense, sick wey; the comedoon's diggin in good style. They wir funny cunts fir that, they flatliners. Anyhow, aw ah wanted tae dae was tae blaw ma muck and git the fuck oot ay thair. That's what ah did, eh. The bird wisnae pleased, but there ye go, needs must. So ye have tae watch oot before ye call it love. It's just another form ay entertainment. See if the feelings transfer tae yir everyday life, then call it love. Love's no jist for weekenders.

– The thing is, Nukes, ah'm changin the keks everyday and cleanin under the helmet.

Nukes raised his eyebrows and smiled, – Must be love then, he said, then he added, – Oan your side, right enough. What's gaun oan wi her though, mate?

12

IT WAS JUST so beautiful, beyond anything ah could have imagined I'd ever feel. It was love no sex. Sex was just the starting motor; this was pure love action. Ah felt her essence, ah know ah did. Ah know she did too, ah know she got there like she'd never done in her life, cause she was greet-in and hiding her face. She felt like she had never been that exposed before. Ah tried tae put my arm around her, but she pulled away. Ah suppose after her sexual problems with the guy she was married to, it was such a big emotional ordeal and she needed time to herself. Ah could dig that, thank fuck I'm a sensitive cunt. Okay, ah said to her softly, okay, I'll gie you some time oan yir ain. It sounded a bit fuckin daft but it was all ah could think of saying. Ah went through to the living-room and put on *Scotsport*: Hibs v. Aberdeen.

She was a bit distant and nippy eftir that, and she went back over tae hers. Ah suppose she just needed time tae git it sorted oot. Ah made up a Bobby Womack tape fae Shaun's collection and took it up tae ma Ma and Dad's.

13

THIS TIME IT was even better than the first time, for me *and* for her. Ah didnae realise it, but ah fucked up big style the first time. She telt me how it felt for her. It was a bit ay a shock. Ah think it's because you always want to get the first one over, there's too much at stake when it's someone you're really intae. The first shag stands alongside yir fledgling relationship like a big question mark, when it's somebody you really care for, really love. Then once you get it oot the road you can settle down tae making love. Things like foreplay can come mair intae their ain. It's funny how there's nae embarrassment aboot stickin yir cock intae a strange lassie, but like licking and caressing her are a bit dodgy the first time. Ah should've got E'd up the first time ah made love tae Heather, eh. E makes it great for strangers, the barriers come down so that sex with a stranger on E is magnificent. See wi someone you love though, the barriers should be down anyway, so the chemicals shouldn't make any difference. Eh, no?

This is what ah want tae discuss with Nukes when he comes up.

Ah make some tea and build a spliff and put on the video of The Orb, the one wi the Dolphins. Keep it psycho-active, there's sex things ah want tae confide in wi Nukes. The spliff is good for Edinburgh soapbar and Nukes is up at my door on cue. Ah've goat ma love tape oan: Marvin, Al Green, The Tops, Bobby Womack, The Isleys, Smokey, The Temptations, Otis, Aretha, Dionne and Dusty. It melts ma fuckin hert, man. Jist git that oan and apply it tae yir ain life n ye'd huv tae be a deid cunt no tae feel as emotional as fuck, eh no. Barry.

– Awright, ma man, Nukes smiles.

– Glad ye came ower, mate, thir was somethin ah wanted tae talk tae ye aboot.

– Aye?

– Ah jist wanted tae see if ye fancied comin up tae McDiarmid Park for the BP Youth game the morn's night. Ally's takin the car, eh.

– Na, cannae be ersed. Snooker tourney doon the club, eh . . . by the way, you cowped that bird yit, Lloyd?

Ah like Nukes, ah lap the cunt up, but see the day? The day ah wish it wis Ally or Amber that had come roond.

14

AH'M SITTIN WI Ally and ah'm telling him: – Ah've never been sae fuckin scared in ma puff, Ally. Mibbee huv tae chill on this relationship thing a bit. It's gittin too heavy.

Ally looks at ays and shakes his heid. – If you run fae this, Lloyd, make sure it's fir the right reasons. Ah see ye when yir wi her. Ah see how ye are. Dinnae deny it!

– Aye, but . . .

– Aye but nowt. Aye but dinnae you start actin the cunt unless thirs something ah dinnae ken. That's aw the fuckin aye buts you need tae listen tae. Dinnae be feared ah love, man, that's what they want. That's the wey they divide. Dinnae ever be feared ah love.

– Mibbe yir right, ah say. – Ye fancy daein some eggs?

Epilogue

I WAS DANCING away at The Pure, kicking like fuck because Weatherall's up from London and he's moved it up seamlessly from ambient to a hard-edged techno dance-beat and the lasers have started and everybody is going crazy and through it all I can see him, jerking and twitching under the strobes and he's seen me and he comes over. He was wearing that top. The one he'd had on when we'd met. The one he put around me that night. – What do you want? I roar at him, not missing a beat.

– Ah want you, he said, – I'm in love with you, he's shouting in my ear.

Easy to say when you're fucking E'd up. But it got to me, and I tried not to show that I was moved, or that he looked so good to me. It had been three weeks. – Yeah, well tell me that on Monday morning, I smiled. It wasn't easy, cause I'm well E'd and feeling so much. I would never be fucked around by a guy again though. Never. The noise was getting to me. It had been so good, but Lloyd had turned it into a grating grind with the piece of shit his simple words implanted in my head.

– I'll be round, he shouted, smiling.

– I'll believe it when I see it, I said. Who the fuck did he think he was.

– Believe it, he said.

Oh Batman, my Dark Fucking Knight I do not think. – Well, I'm away to find Jane, I told him. I had to get away from him. I was on my trip, in my scene. He's a fucking freak, a fucking sad freak. I should have known. I should have been able to tell. Lloyd. Go. I moved to the front of the house. I was trying to get back into the music, thrashing, trying to forget Lloyd, to dance him out of my mind, to get back to where I'd been before he appeared. The crowd are going crazy. This mad guy's in front of Weatherall giving it loads and standing back and applauding as the man responds, taking it higher. I got really hot and breathless and had to stop for a bit. I moved through the mental crowd and hit the bar for some water. I saw Ally, Lloyd's mate. – What's Lloyd on tonight, then? I asked him. I shouldn't have asked him. I'm not interested in Lloyd.

– Nowt, Ally said. He was sweating like he had been really kicking it, – he's just had a couple ay drinks. Didnae want a pill, eh no. Sais eh wis gaunnae take six months oaf n aw that shite. Didnae want ehs perspective damaged, that was what the daft fucker sais. Listen, Heather, man, he says with an air of confidence, – hope yir no gaunnae make him intae a straight-peg, eh.

Lloyd is not E'd up. A thousand thoughts shoot through my head with the MDMA. Weatherall took it down and I started to feel a bit giddy.

– Listen, Ally, I want to ask ye something, I say, touching him lightly on the arm, – Something about Lloyd. I told him what I heard, at that party. All he did was to laugh loudly, slapping his legs before composing himself and telling me the real story.

I felt a bit daft after this. I fingered my second pill which I had taken from my bra and slipped into the watch pocket of my jeans. It was time. But no. I saw Lloyd talking to this guy and these lassies. I nodded to him and he came over. – You talking to anybody special? I asked him, shrinking inside from my own voice: catty, jealous, sarcastic.

He just smiled softly and kept his eyes focused on mine, – Ah am now, he said.

– Want to go? I asked.

I felt his arm slide around my waist and his wet lips make contact with my neck. He squeezed me, and I returned the embrace, standing on my tiptoes, feeling my tits flatten against his chest. After a while he broke off and swept the hair back from my face. – Let's get the coats, he smiled.

We turned our backs on the chaos and headed downstairs.

© Jeffrey Delannoy

IRVINE WELSH was born in the great city of Edinburgh and matured in the housing schemes of Leith, West Pilton and Muirhouse. Neither school nor conventional employment appealed, but he was inspired to write after experiencing the explosions of punk and rave first-hand.

Trainspotting, Welsh's debut novel, was rejected from the Man Booker Prize shortlist, allegedly for offending the judges. It went on to sell over a million copies in the UK alone and was adapted into an iconic film by Danny Boyle, starring Ewan McGregor, Robert Carlyle and Kelly Macdonald. *Porno* was adapted into *T2: Trainspotting*, a sequel that reunited the original cast and crew.

Now the author of twelve novels, most recently *Dead Men's Trousers*, and four books of shorter fiction, Welsh enjoys a dedicated global readership and tweets prolifically, mainly about tennis and corrupt politicians. He serves as the official ambassador of the Homeless World Cup and currently lives in Miami.

RECOMMENDED BOOKS BY IRVINE WELSH:

Trainspotting
Skagboys
Dead Men's Trousers

What do you do when the Rave's over?

Home
SALMAN RUSHDIE

VINTAGE MINIS

Dreams
SIGMUND FREUD

VINTAGE MINIS

Eating
NIGELLA LAWSON

VINTAGE MINIS

Work
JOSEPH HELLER

VINTAGE MINIS

VINTAGE MINIS

The Vintage Minis bring you some of the world's greatest writers on the experiences that make us human. These stylish, entertaining little books explore the whole spectrum of life – from birth to death, and everything in between. Which means there's something here for everyone, whatever your story.

vintageminis.co.uk